Who's n

Baby D lifted the floorboard and grabbed the tiny box hidden underneath. The box in which she'd carefully preserved the remains of her real life. And before she even opened it, Baby D started to cry. But this time her tears weren't full of pain and despair while she helplessly mourned her tragic little death. No. This time, Baby D's tears were full of joy— and the anticipation of her long awaited rebirth.

THERE'S NO PLACE LIKE HOME

THERE'S NO PLACE LIKE HOME

A. G. Cascone

Watermill Press

Copyright © 1997 by Annette Cascone and Gina Cascone.

Cover art by Don Brautigam.

Published by Watermill Press, an imprint and registered trademark of Troll Communications L.L.C.

Printed in the United States of America.

10 9 8 7 6 5 4 3 2 1

For Shirley S. Cascone

Mommy

With love

CHAPTER

1

Baby D stood at the foot of her parents' burning bed crying for her mommy. Her mommy! The mommy who loved Baby D "around the moon and past the stars." The mommy who put all the shiny pink ribbons in Baby D's beautiful long blond hair—just the way Baby D liked them to be. The mommy who played peek-a-boo and pat-a-cake and sang the rabbit song. The mommy who loved Baby D. The mommy Baby D hadn't wanted to lose.

But no one heard Baby D crying for her mommy. Not the lawyer. Or the judge. Or the child psychiatrist who had insisted that Baby D would survive the "trauma" and ultimately be much better off. No. No one ever heard the cries of Baby D— the nameless, faceless, helpless little three-year-old who should never have lost her mommy.

But Baby D wasn't helpless anymore.

Baby D smiled as the painful images of her past started to fade with the sight of her "mommy" and "daddy" being engulfed in the flames. The flames that were now dancing through the room and up the walls. Just the way Baby D had planned.

"Mama!" She spit in disgust as she stood looking down over the bed. "Not in a million years."

With the fire inching its way across the splintered old floorboards, heating the rotted wood under her feet, Baby D savored one last look at the remains of Lorene and Calvin Burnell, satisfied that this "mommy" and "daddy" were finally out of her life for good. As she headed for the door, she comforted herself with the idea that Lorene and Calvin Burnell would be burning forever—in hell, where they both belonged.

Lorene Burnell was not Baby D's "mommy"— no matter how many legal documents the court system had managed to produce. Lorene Burnell didn't even know the meaning of the word. But no one had bothered to find out about that. No one had seemed to care. No one but Baby D.

Calvin Burnell, Baby D's "daddy," wasn't even human as far as Baby D was concerned. But he was definitely lucky. Yeah. Calvin Burnell was real lucky that Baby D recognized the importance of being patient. Otherwise, he would have been dead a long, long time ago.

As the flames billowed out into the hallway behind her, Baby D hurried into the prison cell to which she'd been condemned from the time she was three years old. It was the room the Burnells had given her. The room they said was Baby D's. Only it wasn't. Baby D's room was big and bright and full of lots of wonderful things that always made her happy. This room was cramped and dark and dingy, full of horrible, ugly things that only haunted Baby D. But her sentence here was almost over. Yeah. Within a matter of minutes, Baby D would have at least one fond memory of the room the Burnells had given her—watching it being swallowed up by flames.

Baby D stepped into the bedroom closet—the closet that provided her with the only safe haven she'd ever known in the Burnells' house. Quickly, she pushed aside the piles of dirty clothes that covered the floorboard. The floorboard with the rusty nails that had been rotting out long before Baby D had ever moved in. The floorboard that was so easy for Baby D to pull up, even when she was little.

Baby D lifted the floorboard and grabbed the tiny box hidden underneath. The box in which she'd carefully preserved the remains of her real life. And before she even opened it, Baby D started to cry. But this time her tears weren't full of pain and despair while she helplessly mourned her tragic little death. No. This time, Baby D's tears were full of joy—and the anticipation of her long-awaited rebirth.

Baby D moved to the mirror that hung precariously on the wall above the beat-up old dresser next to the bed as the flames loomed outside her door. But Baby D paid them no attention at all. Instead, she carefully lifted the lid on the box and pulled out the shiny pink ribbon— the one her real mommy had put in her hair. And as she tied it into a bow on the top of her head just the way her mommy used to do it, she smiled. Yeah. Baby D smiled, even though the reflection looking back at her wasn't nearly as perfect as it had been when she was three, and her hair was no longer long and beautiful. But none of that mattered to Baby D now. Because Mommy would fix it. Yeah. Sooner or later, Mommy would fix it all.

Baby D lifted the silver, heart-shaped locket from the box and carefully put it around her neck. It was the locket her mommy always used to wear. The locket with Baby D's picture in it. The one that Baby D would cling to as her mommy cradled her to sleep.

"Baby D will always be in Mommy's heart." The voice that had whispered through her dreams now echoed through her head. But the sound of windows exploding around her quickly drew her thoughts back to reality.

The reality was that Baby D had no intention of burning—at least not yet.

Baby D pulled the blanket from the bed as the flames seized control of the open doorway. Still, Baby D was undaunted. With the blanket draped over her like a hooded cape, Baby D walked calmly through the fire out into the hallway, where she dropped the burning blanket behind her and headed for the stairs.

On the ground floor of the Burnells' house, in the worn-out old rocking chair that stood in front of the filthy, cracked picture window in the "family" room, Baby D sat watching the snow falling outside. She casually brushed away the burning cinders that were falling around her from the ceiling above. And as she rocked back and forth, imagining herself cradled in her mommy's arms again, Baby D sang herself the rabbit song, just the way her mommy used to do.

"In a cabin in the woods . . ."

Behind Baby D, the ceiling in the kitchen came crashing to the floor.

"A little old man by the window stood . . ."

Smoke billowed into the family room, where Baby D continued to sing as if oblivious to it all.

"Saw a rabbit hopping by, knocking at the door . . ."

Baby D took a deep breath, allowing her lungs to absorb the fumes.

"Help me! Help me! The rabbit cried . . ."

White-hot flames roared behind her.

"I just need a place to hide . . ."

Directly above Baby D, the ceiling beams started to give way.

"Come, little rabbit, come inside. I'll take care of you."

Baby D steeled herself against the flames that were now clinging to the bottom of her nightgown. And as she sat with her mommy's locket clutched tightly in her hands, she managed to ease the unbearable pain by concentrating on the words that continued to echo through her head. The words that had comforted Baby D through pains far greater than the ones that she herself had chosen to suffer.

Yeah. Baby D would always be in Mommy's heart. At least, that's what Baby D was counting on.

With the fire tearing through the flannel of her nightgown, searching for her flesh, Baby D ran out of the house onto the snow-covered front lawn— just the way she had planned. And as she threw herself down into the snow, to extinguish the flames and reduce the damage from the burns, Baby D called out for help . . . knowing that no one would ever hear her.

No. No one would ever hear the cries of Baby D. And no one would ever question the tragic deaths of Lorene and Calvin Burnell.

Baby D smiled as she lay watching her past disappear before her very eyes. And before she fell unconscious, one thought ran through her mind.

"Finally . . . Baby D is going home."

CHAPTER 2

"Mom, I'm home," Mallory Dunne called as she stepped through the front door. There was no answer. The house had that quiet, empty feeling. "Mom?"

Kyle Stoddard slipped through the open door behind Mallory. "Looks like there's no one here but you and me," he said.

Mallory closed the door behind him. "Too bad it can't stay that way," she mused.

Kyle headed for the kitchen, carrying the enormous sheet cake that he and Mallory had been sent to pick up. "You're not looking forward to this party at all, are you?"

"I don't know," Mallory said with a shrug, following him. But she did know. She knew when she looked at the balloons, and the streamers, and the lettered banner that read "Welcome Home," and the buffet table, and the cake, that she was most definitely not looking forward to the party that evening.

Kyle put the cake down on the counter and fixed his eyes on her. "What's wrong, Mal?"

She just shook her head, blowing off the question.

"Come on," he pushed. "What is it?"

"You'll think I'm a jerk," she said.

"Me?" He laughed. "Do I have to remind you that I'm the guy who knows that you sucked your thumb until you were eight years old? That you still sleep with a night light? That you peel grapes before you eat them? That in the eighth grade, you kissed Stanley Weiner and promised to marry him?" Kyle paused for dramatic effect. "Need I go on?"

"No." Mallory grinned. "I get the point." The point was that Kyle knew all her secrets—the little, embarrassing ones, and the big, painful ones as well. He knew them and he protected them. And he never thought less of her, or loved her less because of them. Mallory could tell Kyle anything. He was her best friend in the world. And more.

Mallory Dunne and Kyle Stoddard had grown up together. Even before they were born, their parents were best friends. They were even in business together. Their fathers, Ryan Dunne and Michael Stoddard, were land developers who built office buildings, shopping centers, condos, and neighborhoods. The Dunnes and the Stoddards lived in one of those neighborhoods, in two of the nicest houses, on the two biggest lots, right next door to one another.

Their mothers, Joanna Dunne and C. J. Stoddard, ran a large business of their own, a gourmet deli and restaurant called Mom's Place. It was a relatively new business, located in the shopping center that their husbands had built on the edge of their own neighborhood. It was a successful business, but one that was filled with headaches.

Helping their mothers after school, on weekends, and in the summer, Mallory and Kyle had learned quickly that one of the biggest headaches of all was dealing with people. They often joked that the deli was like a magnet for every nut case in the world. If some of the customers were weird, several of the employees were downright scary.

The deli staff was like a Who's Who of hard-luck cases, thanks to Mallory's mother. Joanna Dunne was the quintessential mom, who seemed to think it was her personal responsibility to nurture the world. Mallory couldn't complain really. She got more than her fair share of mothering, nurturing, and love. She knew she was lucky to have her mother, and she was grateful. But every once in a while, she wished that her mother were a little more like Kyle's mother, who let her head rule instead of her heart.

Joanna's heart led her from one worthy cause to another. And her newest was due to arrive shortly. That was the reason for the impending celebration, and Mallory's growing anxiety.

"So tell me what the problem is," Kyle urged.

"I'm just nervous, I guess," Mallory answered.

"Why?" Kyle asked. "You've had exchange students living with you before, and it always turned out okay."

"Yeah, I know," Mallory answered.

"So why are you nervous? Seems to me that this one will be a whole lot easier to deal with, since she speaks English and all."

Mallory laughed. The last two exchange students the Dunnes had hosted were from France, and Mallory and Kyle had had a tough time communicating with them. Mallory's French was limited to the conjugation of three verbs, and Kyle's only reference to the entire country was that Pepé Le Pew, his favorite cartoon character, lived there. In the beginning the language barrier had been a big deal, but that faded as the students learned more English and Mallory learned more French. In fact, Mallory still exchanged letters with both of them, and considered them friends.

"This girl does speak English, doesn't she?" Kyle asked tentatively.

"Of course she does." Mallory shook her head at him, amused. "She's from Detroit. What language do you think she speaks?"

"What do I know?" Kyle shot back.

"It's English, Kyle. Trust me." Mallory laughed.

"So what's the problem then?" he asked.

Mallory didn't have a definite answer. It was more a feeling than anything she could put her finger on. "I don't know." Mallory shrugged. "It's just that the few times I've spoken with her on the phone, she sounds kind of cold. I mean, not rude or anything, just distant. Like she's trying to be nice because she knows she has to be, and not because she really wants to be. You know what I mean?"

"I guess," Kyle said.

"And all she ever wants to talk about is me," Mallory went on. "I swear, she knows more about me than even I do. It's like she's been studying me or something. Like she's going to have to take a pop quiz when she gets here. It's just weird, that's all."

"She's probably just as nervous as you are, Mal." Kyle tried to comfort her. "Probably even more nervous. I mean, look at it from her point of view. She's coming to a strange place, to live with strange people, doing her senior year in a strange high school that's—"

"Full of strange guys," Mallory interjected, teasing Kyle.

Kyle smiled. "You'll probably end up being best friends," he assured her.

Mallory wanted to believe that, but something wouldn't let her. Something told her that tonight was going to be the beginning of a long, hard year.

The front door opened, and her mother's voice called out. "Mallory! Are you home?"

"Yeah, Mom. We're in here," Mallory called back.

"We could use some help bringing the food in."

On their way out to the car, Kyle held open the door for Dee Ann, one of the deli employees who was helping with the party. Dee Ann maneuvered through it, carrying a huge chafing dish full of something that smelled very, very good. She snapped her gum and continued on her way.

"You're welcome, Dee Ann." Kyle shook his head, amused.

Dee Ann Watson was a sight to behold. With her spiked hair, five earrings in each ear, stud in her nose, combat boots, and defiant stance, Dee Ann had an in-your-face attitude that just wouldn't quit. Kyle fondly referred to her as the "rebel without a clue." But Mallory's mom felt sorry for Dee Ann. So for the past several months, Dee Ann had been sometimes a waitress, sometimes a cashier at the deli.

Mallory made a face at her mother as they passed on the front walkway. "Why did you bring Dee Ann to work the party?" she whispered.

"She needed the money," Joanna whispered back, and without further explanation continued into the house.

Of course she needed the money. Dee Ann *always* needed money. That was why she was pinching anywhere from five to forty dollars a week from the cash register. Everybody knew it. But Joanna refused to let Dee Ann be fired. She insisted that Dee Ann was just a lonely and frightened child. While Dee Ann's I.D. gave her age as eighteen, Joanna pegged it closer to sixteen, seventeen tops. Dee Ann bragged that she'd been on her own since she was fifteen, though how or why that had happened, she refused to tell. All anybody knew about her personal life was that she was living with a boyfriend and his mother.

At first, everyone assumed that Dee Ann would be one of those transient workers who came and went before anyone even got around to remembering her name. But Dee Ann had been there for nearly six months and it looked like she was staying.

"She's not so bad," C. J. added as she passed Mallory. C. J. Stoddard was Mallory's second mom, the one who smoothed over misunderstandings and went to bat for Mallory whenever her first mom was being unreasonable.

"She's a nightmare." Carolyn Michaels offered her opinion once C. J. was out of earshot.

Mallory couldn't help laughing and agreeing.

"Every time I have to work with that girl," Carolyn continued, "I keep pinching myself, hoping I'll wake up."

Carolyn had been working at the deli for only a few weeks, and she was having a tough time adjusting to Dee Ann. It was no wonder, Mallory thought. If she had to describe someone who was the complete opposite of Dee Ann Watson, it would be Carolyn Michaels.

Carolyn was the kind of person who fit in no matter where she was. She was so self-assured that she didn't have to do anything to call attention to herself. People paid attention to Carolyn because she made them feel comfortable, about themselves and about her. She was intelligent and had strong opinions about everything, but had a way of expressing her opinions without being confrontational.

Mallory liked Carolyn. And she admired her. Carolyn was about to start her freshman year at the local college. She'd told Mallory that she had to work all through high school just to save enough money to even be able to consider going to a college out of her state. Right now she was living off-campus in a room she'd rented from an elderly couple, because she couldn't afford campus housing. But she didn't seem to mind. On top of signing up for a full course load, Carolyn was working nearly full-time at the deli to help pay her tuition. As far as Mallory was concerned, Carolyn was one of the few "normal" people who worked at the deli. Mallory considered her a real friend.

"Will you look at all this food," Kyle said, peering into the back of his mother's station wagon. "There's enough here to feed an army."

"Yeah," Carolyn agreed. "And I hate to tell you this, but we'd better get a move on, 'cause it's all got to stay warm."

It took several trips to get everything inside. And by then it was time for Mallory and Kyle to leave for the train station to pick up the guest of honor.

"Take your time getting back," Mallory's mother told them. "Drive around town, show her the school. I want to make sure all the guests are here when she arrives."

Mallory's mother had invited half the students in Mallory's class, along with two dozen relatives and friends. When Joanna Dunne decided to throw a party, she did it big.

"Dee Ann." Joanna's attention was diverted. "What are you doing?"

Dee Ann had been lighting the Sterno under the chafing dishes. She stood staring at the last flame, transfixed by it as she ran her finger back and forth through the fire. "Nothing," she answered, continuing to do it.

"Dee Ann, you're going to burn yourself," Joanna chided.

"Nah," Dee Ann told her. "This is just a blue flame. A blue flame's not very hot at all. Fire's not really hot till the flame burns white. That'll roast your skin off. But this flame could barely toast a marshmallow."

"Nonetheless, Dee Ann," Joanna said, "I would really rather you didn't play with fire. With all the other things I have to do tonight, I'm in no mood to make a trip to the hospital."

Dee Ann laughed and withdrew her hand. "Okay. Whatever you say, Mom."

Mom. Mallory felt every muscle in her body tighten. She could swear she even felt her hair clench. She hated when Dee Ann referred to her mother as "Mom." Even though she knew it was absurd, it felt threatening to her. Mallory couldn't figure out why Dee Ann made her feel so possessive about her mother.

"You guys better get going," Joanna said to Mallory and Kyle.

Suddenly, Mallory's feelings about Dee Ann seemed insignificant compared with her growing uneasiness about what was waiting for her at the train station. Like it or not, Mallory's whole life was about to be turned upside down.

CHAPTER

3

Renee Dixon arrived at the station fifteen minutes before her train. She carried her bags down to the platform and made her way to the far end, where she was sure her presence would go unnoticed. When the train arrived, she would simply pick up her bags and slip into the stream of passengers disembarking. That way it would look like she had arrived exactly on schedule—and not three days earlier.

As Renee set her bags down, she was acutely aware of the throbbing in her right forearm. Carrying the heavy bags had caused the cut on the top of her arm to open again. She could feel the sticky wetness inside the bandage, and hoped that she'd done a good enough job dressing the wound that the blood wouldn't seep through and stain her sleeve. She didn't want to have to answer questions about her injury. It was going to be tough enough to explain why she was wearing a long-sleeved blouse in the middle of August.

Renee sat down on the bench and cradled the arm. She should have had stitches, at least a dozen.

But that was out of the question. She'd done the best she could with the injury. Renee had plenty of practice taking care of cuts—and bruises, and burns, and even the occasional broken bone. As Renee gently rubbed her arm, she couldn't help thinking about the time she'd broken it in two places. Well, *she* hadn't broken it, but that's what she'd told the doctor in the emergency room. The story was that Renee had broken her arm in a fall while ice skating. That was a laugh. Renee had never been ice skating in her life. In fact, she had never done much of anything that might be considered fun. But that was going to change.

Renee was free of the past, free of the horror that had been her life, free now to make the rest of her life what she'd always imagined it should be. Nothing was going to stand in her way. There were debts from the past, some of them bigger than others. But she would take care of them all, in her own good time, and in her own way.

Renee watched as more and more people descended onto the platform to wait for the approaching train. It looked like the train would take on as many passengers as it let off. That was good. With all those people milling about, it would be easy for Renee to lose herself in the crowd.

When Mallory Dunne stepped onto the platform, Renee recognized her immediately. Mallory's cover-girl looks made her hard to miss. It was also hard to miss the looks of admiration that Mallory attracted. But Mallory seemed oblivious to it. She was probably so used to that kind of attention, she didn't even notice it.

Renee watched as Mallory ran a hand through her long, blond hair, brushing it back from her face. She reached up to smooth down the short, frizzy strands of her own butchered brown hair. No matter how hard she tried, she couldn't help feeling conscious about her "new look"—the one she'd bought off the shelf of a drugstore for nine-ninety-five. But it was way too late to worry about that now. Besides, in a couple of months the curls would wear out and Renee would grow her hair long again, just like Mallory's.

Renee comforted herself with that thought as she kept a watchful eye on the platform. She was sure Mallory hadn't noticed her. There were enough people, and enough distance and other obstructions between them, that Renee felt comfortably concealed. Besides, Mallory was too involved in her conversation with Kyle Stoddard to be aware of anything or anybody else.

Kyle was as easy to recognize as Mallory was. He was tall and athletic-looking, with dark, wavy hair and strong, perfect features. He looked even better in person than he had in the pictures of him that Renee had seen. Getting a copy of their yearbook had been a stroke of genius. After studying it for weeks, Renee knew all the teachers and all the students. She was determined to fit in as though she really belonged, as though she'd been there all the time.

The blinking light that indicated the arrival of the train told Renee that it was almost show time. She saw Kyle look at his watch, saw both of them glance in the direction of the oncoming train. Kyle put his arm around Mallory reassuringly, and she looked to him for support. Their body language told Renee two things. First of all, Kyle and Mallory were friends, good friends, but not girlfriend and boyfriend. And secondly, this was not a particularly happy occasion for them.

Tough, Renee thought. *It's going to be happy for me.*

The train pulled into the station, and Renee stayed right where she was. If she got up too soon, Mallory might see her, might recognize her from the picture she'd sent to the Dunnes. It was a nice picture, the only one she had with her hair cut short. Renee waited until the platform was sufficiently crowded, and until she was sure that Mallory and Kyle were not looking in her direction, before she stood up and grabbed her bags. Renee moved with the crowd toward the steps where Mallory and Kyle were standing. She could see Mallory standing on tiptoes, craning her neck, looking for her.

As Renee got closer to them, she made a conscious effort to look a little bit lost and forlorn. And she made sure to let Mallory spot her first.

"Renee?" Mallory called from just a few feet away.

Renee looked in their direction, affecting a look of surprise and relief, and headed toward them.

"Renee," Mallory repeated her name. "Hi. I'm Mallory."

"Hi," Renee said, a little timidly. "It's nice to meet you."

"Nice to meet you too." Mallory sounded sincere. "This is my friend Kyle Stoddard."

Renee and Kyle exchanged slightly awkward greetings.

"Here, let me take those for you," Kyle offered, reaching for the heavy bags.

Renee didn't allow herself to wince when he accidentally bumped her arm in the process, sending pain shooting straight to her brain. She just smiled and said, "Thank you."

"So, how was your trip?" Mallory asked as they followed Kyle up the stairs.

"It was okay," Renee answered. "As okay as eighteen hours on a train can be."

"That's right," Mallory said. "You had a long journey."

"You must be exhausted," Kyle added.

"No. Not really. Just a little tired," Renee assured them.

"Too tired to see some of the sights before we head home?" Kyle asked.

"No. I'd like that." Renee forced a smile.

"Great," Mallory chimed in. "Let's swing by Fairmont so that Renee can see the school," she told Kyle.

Renee had already seen the school, along with every other sight in town. Not only had she visited all the important places, she'd been sure to examine them carefully. There were probably a few things about their little town that she could have told them. But she didn't.

Renee sat in the front seat of the car, at Mallory's insistence, as Kyle took the scenic route to the high school, pointing out anything of even marginal interest. He parked in the school parking lot, and they got out to have a look around. Peeking through the windows of the academic building, Kyle and Mallory pointed out the computer rooms, the science labs, and the classrooms of some of their favorite teachers. Then they headed over to the field house and pointed out the indoor, Olympic-sized pool.

Renee made sure to look duly impressed, ooh-ing and ah-ing along the way. She was careful to behave the way an "underprivileged" kid from the inner city who suddenly found herself in the lap of luxury should behave—a little overwhelmed and enormously grateful.

When they got back in the car, Kyle and Mallory continued to fill her in on all the little details about school life. They told her about the best teachers, the best classes, their best friends. Kyle and Mallory were nice enough, and Renee certainly couldn't accuse them of being condescending, but she didn't feel comfortable with them. She couldn't help resenting them, especially Mallory.

"We're almost home," Mallory said when they turned onto Carver Place.

Renee took a deep breath as she spotted the cars parked in front of the house at the end of the cul-de-sac—and all the way down the street, for that matter. *A party!* she realized.

Renee couldn't believe it. A party, just for her. She hadn't had a party in a long, long time. This was starting out even better than she had hoped.

Kyle pulled into the driveway of the enormous brick colonial. "So what do you think?" he asked.

And without thinking, Renee answered, "It's good to be home."

CHAPTER

4

Renee was smooth. She worked the room like a politician, smiling, shaking hands with the adults, and remembering the names of the kids from school with uncanny ease. She was witty and charming, and somehow she managed to say just the right thing to everyone. It was a stunning performance. Renee was in complete control, not only of herself, but of the entire situation. By the end of the evening, everyone liked Renee. Everyone except Mallory.

Mallory berated herself for feeling the way she did, but she couldn't help it, and she couldn't stop it. She stood at the kitchen counter, picking at what was left of the cake, trying to figure out exactly what it was about Renee that bothered her so much.

"Are you going to eat the whole thing?" Her mother's voice snapped her out of her reverie.

Mallory swallowed what was in her mouth, wiped her hands, and smiled sheepishly. "No. I'm done."

"Good." Her mother smiled back at her. "I'd

like to wrap some of it up so Trudy can take it home with her. I hope she'll take some of the food too. I know she hasn't eaten. She didn't take a break all evening. Thanks to her, there's almost no cleanup work to be done. Honestly, I don't know what I'd do without Trudy."

Mallory just rolled her eyes.

Her mother gave her a playful nudge. "Stop it!"

Trudy Zigler was a piece of work. And Mallory could never quite figure out whether she should be terrified of Trudy, or just amused. Trudy was the manager of the deli, and she ran the place like a drill sergeant. Once when Mallory was fifteen minutes late for work, Trudy suspended her for a week. It was what she did to all employees who were more than ten minutes late without a good excuse. The fact that Mallory was the daughter of one of the owners didn't matter one bit to Trudy. Trudy didn't play favorites, and she didn't cut anybody any slack.

Of course, Joanna and C. J. loved Trudy. As far as they were concerned, she was a lifesaver. But even they had to admit that Trudy was a little off. Her style of dress was completely at odds with everything else about her. Trudy was an older woman with the attitude of a marine and the build of a halfback. But her clothes were always soft and frilly, almost childlike. She usually wore pink, and always had a bow in her hair. If she was trying to look feminine, her efforts were having the opposite effect by calling attention to how decidedly *unfeminine* she really was.

"Well, that about does it." Trudy's voice hit the kitchen before she did. "Looks like all the other rooms are shipshape. So I guess I'll be on my way."

"Trudy, I can't thank you enough for all your help," Joanna said as Trudy put the glasses she'd collected from the other rooms into the sink.

"No need to," Trudy said sincerely as she reached for her pocketbook, which was hanging on the back of one of the kitchen chairs. "It was a nice party, huh, girlie?"

"Yeah. It was really nice," Mallory concurred. She didn't take offense at being addressed as "girlie." Not anymore. To Trudy, all the female employees at the deli, including Mallory, were named "girlie." The male employees were simply "hey, you."

"Mal, why don't you go upstairs and see how Renee is doing?" her mother suggested.

Her mother had refused to allow Renee to help clean up after the party. The party was in Renee's honor, after all. Besides, Renee still needed time to unpack and settle in.

Mallory obediently headed out of the kitchen, sauntered through the foyer, and climbed the stairs, in no big hurry to face Renee again. She had no idea what she was going to say, no idea how to open a real conversation with her. It seemed as though she hadn't been able to say the right thing yet. Not that there had been any unpleasantness between them. Renee had been nothing but gracious. But Mallory could see something in her eyes, something that made Mallory sense that Renee didn't like her. She hoped she was just being overly sensitive.

The door to Renee's room was ajar. Renee was sitting on the bed looking at a box she held in her hand. It was a velvet jeweler's box, the kind of box that would hold a necklace. Mallory supposed that was exactly what was in the box. She'd caught only a quick glint of silver before Renee snapped the box shut as soon as Mallory knocked on the door.

"Oh, hi," Renee said a little too cheerfully, as if she'd been caught doing something she wasn't supposed to be doing.

Mallory felt awkward, and unwelcome, as she stepped inside the room. But she made a concerted effort to hide those feelings and to open the lines of communication between her and Renee. "I just wanted to see how you were doing."

"Just fine, thank you," Renee answered politely, as she got up and moved to the dresser. She opened the top drawer and carefully placed the box inside. Then she slid the drawer shut and turned around to face Mallory again, leaning against the drawer as if to protect its contents.

"Is the room okay?" Mallory asked.

"It's beautiful."

Mallory couldn't help noticing that, except for Renee's physical presence, there was no sign of her anywhere in the room. There were no pictures on the dresser, or posters on the walls. No books. No CDs. Nothing. Even her suitcases were out of sight. The room looked exactly as it had before Renee arrived.

"Is there anything you need?" Mallory asked. "Anything I can get for you?"

"I don't think so," Renee answered. "But thank you."

Mallory couldn't think of anything else to say, and Renee wasn't being much help. "Well, I guess you're pretty tired," she said lamely.

"Yes." Renee nodded quickly. "I really am."

"Okay. Well, good night. See you tomorrow."

"Good night." Renee forced a smile.

Mallory stepped back out into the hallway feeling quite rejected, and she didn't think it was her imagination. Nor did she think that Renee's chilly behavior was the result of tiredness. There wasn't even a hint of the warmth that Renee had been spreading around so freely at the party. The Renee that was in that room was very different from the Renee that everyone saw. And Mallory was convinced that it had something to do with her. She just couldn't imagine why.

Mallory reached out to close the door before heading off to her own room. She had her hand on the knob when she stopped herself, remembering that the door had been slightly open when she'd gotten there. Finally, she left it as she had found it, worrying that even the simple act of closing a door might be construed as overstepping her bounds.

Yeah. It was going to be a very rough year.

CHAPTER 5

Welcome home. *What a joke!*
Baby D could barely contain the bile that was rising inside her and the voices that were screaming in her head as she quietly closed and locked the door to the bedroom she had no choice but to occupy—at least for the time being. As she stood there, fighting back angry tears, her mommy's words played inside her mind like a worn-out, scratched-up old record whose melody was barely recognizable anymore. *"Baby D will always be in Mommy's heart."*

How stupid could she be? There was nothing left in Mommy's heart for Baby D. Mommy didn't even recognize her. Because Mommy didn't care about her anymore. No. Mommy didn't have to care about Baby D anymore. Because Mommy had a new baby. A better baby. A baby that she really loved "around the moon and past the stars." A baby she hadn't let anybody take away from her. Baby D was nothing more than a nameless, faceless, helpless little three-year-old that even her mommy had buried with the past.

Baby D covered her ears with her hands, as if that effort alone would silence her brain. "Stop it!" she screamed in a tiny little whisper. "Just stop it!" Her words were barely audible, but the sound of her voice resounded inside her head so loudly, it was as if her words were bouncing off the walls and echoing through the entire house.

For a moment she stood terrified, listening at the door, praying that no one would come, praying that somehow her stupidity would go unnoticed. As the minutes elapsed without any reaction, without even a sound from the hallway outside, Baby D finally felt herself relax.

She even laughed at herself as she headed for the closet to get the duffel bag. She was sure she was just overtired. After all, it wasn't easy to commit a murder *and* attend a party all in the same day. Besides, things were going to work out just as Baby D wanted them to.

Yeah. One way or another, Baby D would have the welcome-home party she really deserved.

Baby D unzipped the duffel bag and carefully pulled out the clump of hair she had wrapped up in the bloodied T-shirt she'd been wearing earlier that day—before the party. It was beautiful hair. Long. And blond. And thick. And Baby D was thrilled to see that most of it was still good. Yeah. Most of it wasn't stained at all.

Carefully, Baby D separated out the strands

that were ruined by blood, dropping them back into the duffel bag with the clothes she planned to reduce to ashes before the night was through. And as she did, Baby D couldn't help thinking that if it hadn't been for Dr. Elaine Baxter, her hair would have been just as beautiful as the hair she was holding in her hands. The hair that belonged to Dr. Baxter's ten-year-old daughter.

Baby D didn't even know the kid's name. She didn't really care. As far as Baby D was concerned, Dr. Baxter's kid was just another nameless, faceless, helpless little thing who didn't deserve to lose her mommy. Which was why Baby D went out of her way to be kind enough to just kill the kid off quickly. That way, she wouldn't have to suffer like Baby D had. Not to mention the fact that there was really no place for Baby D to keep the kid— at least, not alive. Besides, it wasn't about Dr. Baxter's little girl. No. Dr. Baxter's little girl didn't deserve to suffer . . . but her mommy did.

Yeah. Dr. Baxter, the "well-respected" court-certified child psychiatrist whose expert testimony helped sentence Baby D to a fate worse than death, was now going to have to survive a little "trauma" of her own. And Baby D was sure there wasn't enough psychobabble in the entire world to comfort Dr. Baxter the psychiatrist. She would just have to find out the hard way how truly difficult it was for a mommy to lose her baby.

Baby D smiled as she pulled the sandwich-sized Zip-lock storage bag that she'd taken from the Dunnes' kitchen out of her back pocket. "Don't worry about it, Dr. Baxter." Baby D laughed as she dropped the remaining locks of hair into the storage bag. "Ultimately, you'll be much better off."

Baby D grabbed a red felt-tipped marker from one of the jackets she'd thrown into the closet and labeled the front of the bag with the words "Baby B." As she sealed the bag tightly, she couldn't help thinking how easy it was to take away someone's life. But she was much more humane about it than Dr. Baxter had been. Yeah. Taking away someone's life entirely was a whole lot better than forcing them to live one they didn't want.

As Baby D headed for the dresser to get the box—the box where she kept all her important things—she thought about her mommy again. Her mommy . . . and Mallory Dunne. Perfect, sheltered little Mallory Dunne, who had everything that Baby D should have had. Everything that Baby D was going to have.

Yeah. Baby D would always be in Mommy's heart—even if she had to break it before she could piece it back together again . . . the right way.

CHAPTER 6

Trudy Zigler nervously pulled the deli van into the parking spot directly in front of the sliding glass doors that opened into the deli. It was five o'clock in the morning, and Trudy was already running half an hour behind schedule. It wasn't that she was late. The deli didn't open until seven, and Trudy didn't have to punch in until six. But Trudy was a stickler for detail, and getting to work an hour before opening wasn't even close to enough time for her to pull her act together. Particularly this morning.

This morning, on top of all the usual things she needed to accomplish before she felt comfortable enough to open the doors to the public—or to the other employees for that matter—Trudy had to find a way to clean out the back of the van. Preferably while it was still dark—and definitely before anybody arrived.

She had planned to clean it out the night before. But by the time she left the party at the Dunnes' house, she was more than exhausted. By the time Trudy got home and up to her room, it was well past midnight, three and a half hours after the time she normally retired. And while she knew she was playing with fire by pushing herself so hard, Trudy had every intention of cleaning out the van at twelve-thirty in the morning when she stepped into her closet to hang up her clothes.

The problem was, Trudy hadn't made it out of her closet until the alarm clock started screaming at her hours later, a little less than an hour before she had planned to get to work. By the time Trudy had gathered her wits and realized where she was, she was more irritated than upset by the fact that she had obviously passed out again.

Trudy Zigler was used to her "little spells." Until recently, they seemed to be under control. Trudy had been suffering from these spells ever since she was a child. Over the years, at the urging of her mom—her *real* mom—Trudy had been through a series of CAT scans and MRIs and had allowed more blood to be drawn from her body than even Dracula would have wanted to consume. But nobody had ever found the cause.

The doctors chalked it up to stress and to the trauma she'd suffered as a child. While Trudy thought it was all nonsense, she made a conscious effort to follow their advice and maintain a daily regimen of proper diet and exercise. But whatever it was that caused her "little spells" was still an unsolved mystery, one that Trudy could have lived without—particularly last night.

Trudy reached under the seat to grab the lockbox where she kept her handgun. The gun no one knew she had. While she felt a little guilty sneaking it in and out of work every day, given how adamant Joanna and C. J. had been at the mere suggestion of keeping a firearm in the store for protection, Trudy was not about to leave home without it. Trudy was an expert at handling knives—thanks to her, the deli had a full supply of sharp, high-quality knives—but she knew that in a clinch, there was nothing easier to use than a gun.

Trudy threw the gun into her purse, got out of the van, and walked to the side door. Once she was inside, she had sixty seconds to get to the alarm and enter her code to disarm the "security system" Joanna and C. J. had installed. She did it in fifteen. Time was ticking away, and Trudy had none to spare.

Quickly, she headed for the two sliding glass doors in the center of the store so she could drag in the stacks of newspapers that were sitting out front. It was the first thing she did every morning, even though Joanna had told her to wait for one of the guys to show up to help her. But that was a waste of time: Trudy was perfectly capable of doing it herself.

Stack by stack, Trudy started sliding the three hundred pounds of papers through the open doors onto the tiled floor of the deli. Because the van cleanup was still weighing heavy on her mind, she managed to get them all inside in half the time it usually took her. The deli carried almost every paper New York and Philadelphia had to offer, as well as both local publications, at the suggestion of Trudy, who insisted the papers alone would bring in more morning traffic. And they did. But today Trudy was sorry she'd ever opened her mouth. Because today she could definitely have used the additional time to hose down the back of the van.

Even before she sliced open the heavy plastic strapping that bundled *The Packet,* one of the town's local papers, the headline immediately caught her eye. "Ten-year-old Daughter of Prominent Psychiatrist Missing." Trudy pulled the top paper off the stack. Without looking at the name beneath the picture on the front page next to the article, Trudy knew whose daughter it was.

Yeah. Trudy Zigler knew all about Dr. Elaine Baxter. And she wasn't at all surprised by the fact that *The Packet* had run Dr. Baxter's picture on the cover instead of her daughter's. It was probably Dr. Baxter's suggestion, Trudy thought. She considered Dr. Baxter nothing more than a cold-hearted, status-conscious, publicity-seeking, incompetent psycho who was in desperate need of some therapy herself.

Trudy scanned the article quickly, amused to

see that it cited more details about Dr. Baxter's "prominent career" than it did about the disappearance of her daughter. Maybe it was because Dr. Baxter enjoyed the publicity—even through her own trauma.

Trudy slid *The Packet* aside and cut into the last stack of papers. As she removed the plastic wrapping of *The Times,* the better of the two local publications, Trudy was pleased to see that at least somebody was reporting the case responsibly. There was no mention on the front page of *The Times* of a "prominent psychiatrist." Just the picture of a beautiful little girl with long blond hair who was "missing."

Trudy liked *The Times* and thought it did an excellent job of reporting. Particularly in the articles about Baby D. Yeah. *The Times* had done a real number on Dr. Elaine Baxter during the Baby D trial—without the use of a firearm. Trudy got a real kick out of it too. It was just a shame that even *The Times* couldn't save Baby D.

Trudy was dying to read both articles carefully, but it would have to wait until later. Quickly, she threw the remaining papers up onto the shelves and headed for the register to pay for the two papers she was planning to keep.

Then Trudy Zigler reset the security alarm and headed back out of the deli to clean up the blood in the back of the van.

CHAPTER 7

"Are you people eating breakfast or lunch?" Dee Ann asked, cracking her gum as she dropped a stack of menus on the table in front of Mallory. "'Cause if you're eatin' breakfast, you better order fast. You're the only table in the place, and the kitchen's gettin' ready to switch over. I'm in no mood to listen to Dennis chew my head off for puttin' in an egg order after he puts all the breakfast crap away."

"Good morning to you too, Dee Ann," Kyle said as he reached for a menu. "Dee Ann won the deli's Miss Congeniality Award last month," Kyle told Renee. She was sitting across the booth from him, next to Mallory. "As a matter of fact," Kyle went on, "if you're thinking about working here during the school year, you'll probably have to train with Dee Ann. Dee Ann's got the whole employee handbook memorized, especially the section on prompt and courteous customer service."

Mallory laughed. But Renee didn't.

"Bug off," Dee Ann said. She popped the bubble she'd blown, then turned and walked away.

"He's only kidding," Mallory told Renee, who was still sitting there, looking confused. Or offended. Mallory couldn't really tell which. "We don't really have a Miss Congeniality contest," she went on. "And if you decide you want to work here, Dee Ann is definitely the last person in the place Trudy would have you train with."

Renee smiled politely.

"The employee handbook is really just a few rules Trudy threw together," Mallory tried again.

This time Renee didn't even bother to respond.

Besides lacking a warm and sunny disposition, at least around Mallory, it was quite clear that Renee lacked a sense of humor as well. There were only a few seconds of silence, but it felt so uncomfortable, Mallory wanted to scream. Renee had been in Mallory's life for less than twenty-four hours, and already it felt way too long.

"So." Kyle's voice cut through the tension. "Do you think you might want to work here?"

Mallory was hoping with all her heart that Renee would say no. On top of having to live with the girl seven days a week, Mallory was going to have to go to school with her too. And given that Renee had signed up for all of the same classes Mallory was taking, Mallory was sure that at least five days a week, eight hours a day, there'd be no way of escaping Renee.

"Yeah." Renee's answer dashed any hopes

Mallory had. "I think I'd really like to work here. I wouldn't even mind training with Dee Ann."

Kyle smiled.

Mallory could tell that Kyle's smile was just as forced as her own. Renee's tone suggested that she was kidding about Dee Ann, but the look in her eyes suggested something quite different. Mallory felt incredibly uncomfortable. It was as if Renee was berating them for picking on Dee Ann.

"She's a character, all right," Kyle said awkwardly.

"Yeah, well, in some of the restaurants in my old neighborhood," Renee told him, "Dee Ann really *would* win Miss Congeniality."

"There you are," Joanna Dunne said, saving Mallory from having to reply. "Did you guys order yet?"

"No," Mallory answered as her mother sat down next to Kyle.

"I'm sorry I didn't have a chance to make breakfast for you myself this morning," Joanna said to Renee. "But I wanted to let you sleep. Plus C. J. and I had a bunch of errands to do. So I hope you'll forgive me."

Renee smiled. "I'm sorry I slept so late, Mrs. Dunne."

"Oh, no, honey," Joanna said. "That's not what I meant." She patted Renee's hand. "You could have stayed in bed all day if you wanted to. I'm just sorry that I didn't have the time this morning to make your first breakfast here a nice one at home."

"After all the trouble you went through for me last night," Renee told her, "I'm sorry I didn't have a chance to make breakfast for *you* this morning, Mrs. Dunne."

Mallory wanted to puke.

Joanna smiled. "Please, call me Joanna."

"Hey, Mom," Dee Ann greeted Joanna as she stepped back up to the table with a whole new attitude.

"Or Mom." Joanna smiled at Renee before she looked up at Dee Ann.

Mallory cringed. She knew her mother was just kidding, but she wasn't sure that Renee knew that, because as Joanna turned away, Renee grinned from ear to ear, just like a Cheshire cat.

"Has everyone decided what they'd like to order?" Dee Ann asked in her most professional waitress tone. "Or shall I make some suggestions?"

Kyle laughed. "I thought you already did."

Dee Ann shot him a dirty look.

"If you like omelets," Joanna told Renee, "we make some really good ones."

"We sure do," Dee Ann agreed, suddenly unconcerned with the idea of putting in an egg order at the last minute.

"Are you sure Dennis hasn't put all the 'breakfast crap' away?" Kyle needled.

Dee Ann shot him another look.

"Kyle," Joanna said, sounding amused. "There's still half an hour before lunch. And we don't serve breakfast 'crap.'"

Mallory had to stifle a laugh as she watched Dee Ann sweating out the moment, waiting to see if Kyle would rat on her. Kyle loved tormenting Dee Ann. And Mallory loved watching it, especially now, when Dee Ann was really trying to act like Miss Congeniality for Joanna's benefit.

Finally he let Dee Ann off the hook. "All the breakfast stuff is really good," he said to Renee.

"An omelet sounds great," Renee told Dee Ann.

"Are you eating?" Dee Ann asked Joanna, before she even acknowledged Mallory.

"No," Joanna answered. "But you can bring me a cup of coffee."

By the time Dee Ann finally managed to get their orders straight and on the table, Mallory was almost too nauseated to eat from Renee's saccharin-covered conversation with Joanna and C. J., who had joined them as well.

Renee was clearly a showman when the audience was important. And she was definitely running the show. She complimented Joanna and C. J. on everything from their successful home lives to their successful business, asking one question after another about how they managed to accomplish both. Joanna and C. J. seemed to be eating it up almost as enthusiastically as Renee was devouring her "delicious" omelet.

By the time the dishes were cleared, Renee had won herself a five-star review. Mallory couldn't help feeling a little bit unnerved at how smooth Renee could be when she wanted to.

"Hey, girlie." Trudy's voice attracted the attention of every female employee in the place, including Joanna and C. J. "You're nine and a half minutes late."

Trudy was following Carolyn, who was heading through the restaurant toward the waitress station carrying an armful of pink papers. Trudy's voice stopped her dead in her tracks, two tables in front of them.

"I'm really sorry, Trudy," Carolyn apologized. "I won't let it happen again."

"Yeah." Trudy was unrelenting. "Well, you've got a thirty-second grace period to explain to me why it happened now. And if it isn't a darn good, break-my-heart kind of a reason, I might bend my own rules and suspend you anyway. 'Cause for all I know, that clock up there's running thirty seconds slow."

While Trudy didn't really have an employee handbook, the ten-minute-late rule was first on the list that she did have. Second on her list was her understanding with Joanna and C. J. that when it came to the employees, she ran the ship. So while

Mallory shot her mother and C. J. a pleading look to save Carolyn, Joanna and C. J. sat quietly. The rules were the rules. Even Joanna and C. J. were afraid to break them.

"I was at the student center at the university to register for classes." Carolyn started to plead her own case. "While I was there, a cop came in with a bunch of these flyers to ask the students to put them up around campus." Carolyn showed Trudy the stack of papers in her hands. "They're about that little girl who's missing. It was in all the papers this morning."

Trudy's rigid drill-sergeant expression changed immediately.

"The cops have people out all over the county putting them up," Carolyn continued. "So when I offered to bring some here to see if maybe we could pass them out to the customers, he thought it was a great idea. But he had only a small stack left with him. By the time I followed him back to his car for more, I was running over the time I'd figured it would take me to register and get to work."

Mallory smiled. Carolyn definitely had a "darn good, break-my-heart kind of reason" for being late. And it was quite clear by the look on Trudy's face that she was going to accept it.

"Okay, girlie." Trudy's voice softened. It even sounded a little shaky, like she'd been caught off guard. "I'll let it go this time."

"Is it okay to pass these out?" Carolyn asked.

Trudy glanced over at Joanna. "That's not a decision for me to make," Trudy told Carolyn. "You'll have to ask one of the owners."

Mallory almost started to laugh. How was it that Trudy could make the decision to fire an employee or not right on the spot, but she couldn't make a decision about passing out flyers to help find a missing little girl? The woman definitely had a couple of screws loose.

Carolyn headed for the table, with Trudy right behind her.

"Trudy said that I should ask you if it's okay to pass out these flyers," Carolyn said as she set the stack down on the table. "To help find the little girl who's missing."

Mallory stared at the picture of the smiling little girl on the flyer. She was sure that wherever the little girl was now, she wasn't smiling. She was probably terrified. "That's so sad," Mallory sighed.

"Isn't it?" Carolyn agreed. "I just hope nothing horrible has happened to her."

"Don't bank on it," Dee Ann chimed in. "Ten-year-old kids don't just run away by themselves. Somebody took her. And a bunch of flyers aren't gonna do squat to save that kid from the terrible thing that's probably already happened to her."

Mallory shook her head in disgust. Dee Ann was more than obnoxious—she was cruel.

CHAPTER

8

Joanna couldn't take her eyes off the picture of the beautiful little girl on the flyer. But her thoughts weren't with that little girl. They were somewhere else, with another beautiful little girl. A little girl who was lost forever. A little girl who was never coming home to her mommy.

Joanna's heart cramped. The pain seemed fresh and new again, even though so many years had passed. Time had done nothing to heal the wound. In some ways, the passage of time made it hurt all the more. It was horrible to think how long it had been since Joanna had last set eyes on that precious baby girl.

"Baby D." That's what they called her in court and in the press. The trial was a media circus—and a personal tragedy.

Joanna could still remember the morning they'd come to take her away. It was 9:00 A.M. when two sheriff's deputies arrived, accompanied by Dr. Elaine Baxter, the press, and dozens of onlookers. It was as if the grim reaper had arrived, as if they were surrendering the three-year-old baby to death.

Because once they handed her over, once she left the house, she was gone for good, never to be seen or heard from again. That was the court's decision.

It was a decision that Dr. Elaine Baxter supported. A decision that Dr. Elaine Baxter helped bring about. And a decision that Dr. Elaine Baxter executed, because in the end, it was Dr. Elaine Baxter who tore the screaming child from her mother's arms. She did it without apology, without remorse.

Dr. Elaine Baxter was so sure that she was right. She was so sure that Baby D belonged with Lorene and Calvin Burnell, she convinced the court, most of the press, and the majority of the public of that as well.

But she did not convince Joanna Dunne. Nothing in the world would ever convince Joanna. In her heart she knew that Lorene and Calvin Burnell could never give that baby the life she deserved.

Joanna prayed every day for Baby D. Prayed that she was safe and sound somewhere . . . and happy. It was torture not knowing. Losing a child was the worst torture in the world.

Now you know, Joanna thought bitterly. *Now you know.* But there was no comfort in that thought. Joanna did not want Elaine Baxter to suffer that way. It was an agony that Joanna wouldn't wish on her worst enemy.

"Poor little girl," Kyle said.

"Poor mother," C. J. added, giving voice to Joanna's own thought.

"Yes," Joanna agreed, looking C. J. right in the eye. "Poor mother."

Joanna took comfort from the strength in C. J.'s eyes. C. J. Stoddard was the strongest woman Joanna had ever known. She loved C. J., admired her, and relied upon her.

The two women had been best friends since college. They'd been together through the best of times, and the worst. Without question, the worst was the "Baby D" trial.

But shortly after it was over there was the miracle. Both Joanna and C. J. found out, within weeks of one another, that they were pregnant. No babies had ever been more wanted. Or more needed. C. J. had an easy pregnancy, but Joanna had trouble right from the start. By the third month she was bedridden, and there was little hope that the child would make it to term.

C. J. took care of Joanna. She was with her every day while their husbands were at work. It was as if C. J. had every bit as much invested in that baby as Joanna did. Even now, Mallory was as much a daughter to C. J. as she was to Joanna. And Kyle was as much a son to Joanna as he was to C. J.

Joanna looked at their children, their beautiful, healthy, happy children. She couldn't bear the thought of ever losing one of them. Suddenly, her heart ached for Dr. Elaine Baxter. Joanna was surprised that she could feel genuine compassion for the woman who had caused so much pain.

"Let's put these flyers on the front counter," she told C. J.

C. J. nodded her agreement. "Let's hope this mother's child comes home to her."

CHAPTER 9

Baby D could feel the blood rushing through her veins as she watched Joanna and C. J. head toward the front counter with the stack of pink flyers. The flyers that provided Baby D with a perfect opportunity to see her mommy's reaction to the carefully coordinated and brilliantly executed little trauma that Dr. Elaine Baxter was now suffering. Yeah. The flyers were a stroke of luck. But the reaction Baby D witnessed was not the reaction she was hoping for.

Poor mother!

Baby D wanted to scream as she tried to silence the little three-year-old's voice that was crying out inside her. *Poor mother!* How could her mommy even begin to feel for that monster?

Dr. Elaine Baxter deserved to suffer a fate worse than death. She deserved to spend the rest of her days tortured by the pain and guilt and despair that the loss of her child would surely cause. It was Dr. Baxter's own fault. Didn't Baby D's mommy see that? Didn't her mommy understand?

Baby D's heart clenched as she watched her mommy hesitate for a moment by the trash container behind the front counter. And for a second, Baby D was sure that her mommy was going to pitch the flyers right into the garbage where they belonged. How stupid could she be? Of course her mommy had to pretend to worry about Dr. Baxter's little girl! What else could she do? Blow up balloons and throw a big deli party?

But Baby D's mommy didn't throw the flyers away. No. The flyers ended up on the front counter for all the customers to see.

Every muscle in Baby D's body contracted with rage as she forced a polite smile in response to the pathetic little conversation that was going on around her. And as she watched Mallory Dunne run her perfectly manicured fingers through her perfect, silky blond hair, exchanging perfectly petty remarks with Kyle Stoddard, her perfect male counterpart, she thought about rendering yet another trauma on Dr. Elaine Baxter. Yeah. It would be nice to rip out Dr. Elaine Baxter's innards so that she wouldn't ever have the chance to replace *her* "lost" baby with a better one.

Baby D glanced back at her mommy as the anger inside her swirled around the pain that was rising like a tidal wave. Yeah. From the time she was torn from her mother's arms, anger and pain were the only emotions Baby D had ever known.

Most times, Baby D couldn't even distinguish between the two. As she dug her fingernails into the palms of her clenched fists in an effort to hold back the tears, every nerve ending in her body ached for her mommy's touch.

Baby D was the better baby! Because Baby D loved her mommy "around the moon and past the stars!" And no other baby would ever love her mommy that much!

Baby D's mommy was right. Dr. Elaine Baxter really was a "poor mother." Because Dr. Elaine Baxter's baby was never coming back. No. Dr. Elaine Baxter wasn't anywhere near as lucky as Baby D's mommy. Baby D's mommy didn't know it yet. But she would. Yeah. Piece by piece, Baby D was going to put their lives back together again.

Pretty soon, Baby D's mommy would find out just how much "around the moon and past the stars" really meant.

CHAPTER 10

Shortly after Joanna and C. J. walked away, the table grew quiet. Conversation about the missing child had been exhausted, but everybody seemed reluctant to bring up another topic. It was as if going on to a happier subject was somehow insensitive, disrespectful even.

But as Mallory sat there silently, she noticed something that made her smile. It was something she'd noticed before, but she hadn't known quite what to make of it then. Now she was sure.

Mallory knew she was staring, but she wasn't self-conscious about it. In fact, she was hoping to get caught. She waited for Carolyn's eyes to meet hers, but that didn't happen. Carolyn's eyes were fixed on someone else.

Mallory had suspected for some time that Carolyn had a crush on Kyle. She had caught her stealing glances at him more than once. But the way that Carolyn was looking at Kyle now, as if he were some kind of god, finally proved Mallory's suspicions beyond a shadow of a doubt.

Mallory couldn't have been happier, because

she knew that Kyle had a crush on Carolyn. He'd told Mallory as much. But he'd also told her that he just didn't have the guts to ask Carolyn out. And it didn't look as though Carolyn was going to make the first move either. It was up to Mallory to find a way to push the two of them together.

"Hey, girlie." Trudy's voice cut through the deli like one of the sharp knives that no one was allowed to touch.

All heads turned. Even Renee's. When Trudy talked, everybody listened.

"If you want to get paid for your time, you'd better clock in," Trudy told Carolyn.

Carolyn left the table immediately to do as she was told.

Mallory took the opportunity to excuse herself to go to the ladies' room. She walked through the restaurant, around the front counter, and toward the rear of the deli. But when she got to the ladies' room, she walked right past it, pushing open the two swinging doors that led to the back of the store. She found Carolyn standing by the time clock, punching her time card.

"Hey, Mal." Carolyn smiled. "What are you up to today?"

"Nothing much," Mallory answered. "Just showing Renee around."

"That's nice," Carolyn said.

Mallory just shrugged. She had something else

on her mind, something much more important. "Mind if I ask you a personal question?" she asked Carolyn.

"Shoot." Carolyn laughed.

"Are you interested in Kyle?" Mallory blurted out.

Carolyn had guilt written all over her face. "Uh . . . why do you ask?" she stumbled over the words.

Mallory thought it was sweet the way Carolyn and Kyle were so nervous about liking each another. Sweet and silly. As far as Mallory was concerned, the two of them were perfect together.

"Oh, just little things I've noticed," Mallory responded to Carolyn's question.

"Such as?"

"Such as the way you're always looking at him," Mallory said, grinning.

"Am I?" Carolyn asked, sounding a little alarmed.

"Yes," Mallory answered. "But don't worry about it, because I happen to know that he's interested in you too."

"What?" Carolyn looked stunned. "How do you know that?"

"He told me," Mallory replied. "So now what are you going to do about it?"

"I don't know," Carolyn said, fumbling to replace her time card in its slot. "I have to think about it."

"Why don't you ask him out?" Mallory suggested.

"Yeah, right." Carolyn laughed, turning red.

"I'm telling you," Mallory pushed, "the two of you would be perfect together."

"I'll think about it, okay?" Carolyn appeased her. Then she quickly changed the subject. "So how are you getting along with Renee?"

Mallory let out a heavy sigh.

"Not so well, huh?" Carolyn asked. "Don't you like her?"

"I get the feeling she doesn't like *me*," Mallory answered. "Not one bit. And I don't know why."

"Why don't you just come right out and ask her about it?" Carolyn said. "You know, clear the air. You've got to live with this girl for a whole year. You'll go nuts if you don't find a way to make things pleasant between you."

"I don't think talking to her will help," Mallory said hopelessly. "She won't be straight with me. She's just not a very up-front person, not the kind of person you can just come right out and say things to."

"Like me, you mean," Carolyn joked.

Mallory smiled. "Exactly. I know I can say anything to you," she told Carolyn.

"That's good," Carolyn said. "At least I think so." She headed for the swinging doors that led to the deli. "I've got to get to work or Trudy will have my head."

As they walked through the doors, they practically ran into Renee.

"Renee," Mallory gasped, surprised by Renee's sudden appearance. At least Mallory hoped her appearance was sudden. She hoped that Renee hadn't been standing there listening to her conversation with Carolyn. "What are you doing back here?" She tried to sound a little less startled.

"I was just waiting to use the bathroom," she explained simply. "The door was locked, so I thought you were in there."

Mallory tried the door, realizing too late that her action made it appear that she didn't believe Renee. But she didn't. And the fact that the door *was* locked didn't really change her mind.

"Somebody may have locked the door on their way out by mistake," Carolyn said, knocking on the door. There was no answer. "It happens all the time." She knocked again. Still no answer. "I'll go get the key." Carolyn walked away, leaving Mallory standing there alone with Renee.

Mallory struggled to find something to say that would fill the uncomfortable silence between them. But there was more than silence that stood between Mallory and Renee. Much more. But Mallory hadn't the vaguest idea what it was. She was pretty sure of one thing though. Renee *had* overheard her conversation with Carolyn. It was written all over her face.

Mallory couldn't help feeling uneasy, especially since the expression on Renee's face looked a lot more like anger than hurt or humiliation.

Mallory wanted to say something, but she was afraid that she would just make things worse. She finally decided to just excuse herself, breaking away from Renee's icy glare. "I guess I'll go back to the table."

Renee nodded. But she never took her eyes off Mallory.

Even as she walked away, Mallory could feel Renee watching her. She glanced over her shoulder to see if she was right. Renee *was* watching. And if looks could kill, Mallory figured that she'd be dead on the spot.

CHAPTER 11

*S*o this is the house that Jack built.

Baby D wanted to retch as she sat in the car across the street from Jack Riley's enormous, two-story colonial. It sat on at least two acres of perfectly landscaped property, built on the foundation he stole from Baby D.

Yeah. Thanks to Baby D, Jack Riley was living the good life. And Baby D was pretty sure he couldn't care less about the life he had sacrificed in the process.

Jack Riley's "brilliant prosecution" of the Baby D case didn't cost the Burnells a dime. Jack Riley took the case *pro bono*, for free, knowing full well that winning a case as controversial as Baby D's would guarantee him the kind of future he argued was inconsequential for Baby D.

Jack Riley managed to reduce the Baby D trial to a war of the classes, between the "haves" and the "have nots," as if the only question to be answered was whether money alone should decide a child's fate. And while Baby D's entire life hung in the balance, Jack Riley managed to sway a judge, a jury, and public sympathy over to the painful plight of the "have nots," insisting that Lorene and Calvin Burnell's "wealth" lay in their overwhelming desire to love and nurture their own biological child.

It was a brilliant argument. But it was a lie. And Jack Riley knew it. Yeah. Jack Riley knew that "have nots" didn't even begin to describe Lorene and Calvin Burnell. Jack Riley knew that the Burnells were devoid of a whole lot more than money. But it didn't matter to him. For Jack Riley, one baby's tragedy was just another man's triumph.

But today the shoe was on the other foot. Yeah. Today, one man's tragedy would be just another little triumph for Baby D.

Baby D watched as the youngest of Jack Riley's children headed down the driveway riding a shiny new two-wheeler with yellow and white streamers hanging from the handlebars. It was the kind of bike Baby D always wanted. Only Baby D would have chosen pink and purple streamers instead. But thanks to Jack Riley, not only did Baby D never get any love or nurturing, she never got a bike either.

Baby D followed the little girl down the street, careful to stay a safe distance behind, until she realized the kid was heading toward the park at the other end of the block. Yeah. Someone up there was on Baby D's side. Jack Riley's little girl was making things easy.

Baby D passed the bike, keeping her eye on the kid in the rear-view mirror until the bike turned onto the dirt path that led to the playground. Mercifully, the playground was deserted. Baby D stepped on the gas and headed around the block to leave the car on the other side of the park, near the woods.

Show time was about to begin.

Baby D pulled the leash out of the bag on the seat next to her, ripped off the price tag, opened the car door, and headed through the woods toward the playground. She began calling for "Snowball," her "missing puppy."

Yeah. The "missing puppy" routine had worked like a charm on Dr. Elaine Baxter's kid. Baby D thought it was a hoot. The kid never hesitated, never even thought twice about following Baby D. The "brilliant child psychiatrist" apparently wasn't brilliant enough to teach her own child about the danger of talking to strangers. In fact, the kid was so gullible, Baby D could have lured her to her death with just a pocket full of candy.

"Snowball!" Baby D called out again, as she stepped out of the woods, dragging the leash behind her.

Jack Riley's little girl turned toward the sound of Baby D's voice.

Baby D headed in the direction of the swing set, looking terribly worried. "Have you seen a little furry white puppy roaming around here?"

Baby D asked, as her eyes scanned the park looking for any other signs of life.

Jack Riley's little girl shook her head.

"Are you sure?" Baby D asked, feigning concern.

The kid shook her head again.

"I can't believe this," Baby D sighed to herself, deliberately turning her back on the kid as she stepped away from the swing set. "Snowball!" She called out toward the woods. "Where are you?"

"Your puppy ran away?"

Baby D smiled to herself, then turned back around, looking as sick with worry as a parent with a missing child. "I hope not," Baby D answered. "I knew I shouldn't have let him off the leash," she mumbled. "He likes to run around a lot, but the last time I let him go, he came right back when I called him. Only this time, I've been calling and calling, and he's just not coming." Baby D cried out for the imaginary missing puppy again. "I'll die if anything has happened to him," she told the kid. "He's just a baby, you know?"

Jack Riley's little girl got off the swing, looking as anxious as Baby D was pretending to be. "If you want, I can try to help you find him."

Bingo.

"I'd really appreciate it." Baby D smiled her gratitude to the kid for being just as gullible as

Elaine Baxter's little girl. "He likes to play in the woods back here," she told her. "He likes chewing on sticks and stuff."

"My dog used to chew on everything when he was a puppy," Jack Riley's little girl said.

Baby D smiled. And as she spewed out some inane chit-chat about "Snowball," Jack Riley's little girl followed her right into the woods.

Yeah. The "missing puppy" routine was definitely a winner.

It worked like a charm.

CHAPTER

12

Renee was stuck in rush-hour traffic, at a complete standstill. She could see the bridge that crossed the river, and state lines, up ahead. Once she made it over the bridge, she was fifteen minutes from home. The problem was that she was already two hours late. Time sure flies when you're having fun.

Renee was concerned more about appearances than about consequences. There would be no consequences. Renee had her alibi in place. Joanna would be perfectly understanding.

Mallory, on the other hand, would be pretty ticked-off. But Renee didn't really care. Mallory had been ticked-off even before Renee left for her big adventure. Mallory had tried to hide it, tried to be a sport about it. But Renee could tell that Mallory wasn't the least bit happy that Joanna offered to let Renee borrow Mallory's car without even asking Mallory first. Renee was sure that the only reason Mallory let it slide was because she'd be getting rid of Renee for the whole day.

Joanna wasn't terribly comfortable with the

idea at first, not until Renee convinced her that she would appreciate a little time to herself. She told Joanna that she was going shopping, that she wanted to buy herself something to wear on the first day of school. Something appropriate. Something that would make her fit in.

Joanna understood. She even offered to let Renee use her credit card. Renee thanked her but politely declined Joanna's "generous" offer. Renee said that she just couldn't allow herself to take Joanna's credit card. What Renee didn't tell Joanna was that the reason she couldn't take the card was because she wasn't really going shopping.

But Joanna would never know that. Sitting on the seat next to Renee was a shopping bag full of brand-new clothes, with the tags still attached. Renee had bought them on her second day in town, twenty-four hours before Mallory picked her up at the train station. She knew the clothes would come in handy, knew they would provide her with a good excuse to get away by herself for a while.

Renee had several excuses lined up that would allow her time alone. Because Renee knew that she was going to need time alone to do what she had to do without having to make explanations to anybody else. Today had been one of those times.

The fact that she was going to be more than two hours late getting back wouldn't be a problem either. She would just apologize and say that she lost track of time. Maybe she'd even tell them that she got lost. That by itself could account for close to an hour. And it wouldn't hurt in the sympathy department either. It would also account for the huge difference in the odometer reading.

According to the odometer, Renee had traveled more than a hundred miles that day. But Renee was pretty confident that nobody would notice. Nobody ever looked at the odometer. And if she was wrong, if Mallory did notice how far Renee had gone and questioned her about it, Renee would simply be forced to tell her that she had spent the day at the zoo.

She could just picture their faces when she laid that on them. They'd stand there dumbfounded, trying not to laugh. But by the time Renee was done with them, they'd be trying not to cry. She'd hit them with a real sob story. The poor, underprivileged kid was too embarrassed to admit that she'd never been to a zoo before. So she snuck off by herself so that no one would have to feel sorry for her. And if they didn't believe that, she'd show them the plastic zoo key she had, the one that made all those talking boxes work. Now that was pathetic. A real "break-my-heart kind of story."

But pathetic just wasn't Renee's style, and she was pretty sure she wouldn't have to resort to it.

The traffic inched forward, but Renee was so

lost in her thoughts that she didn't notice at first. She stood still a moment too long, and the driver behind her blared his horn, as if moving up that extra couple of feet would get him home any faster.

Renee was about to thrust her arm out the window and give the jerk one of her favorite crude gestures. That was precisely the thing to do in her old neighborhood. But Renee caught herself in time. She reminded herself that she was not in the old neighborhood. Not anymore. Not ever again.

Besides, there was no reason to give in to hostility. Not when her plans were all working out so perfectly.

CHAPTER

13

Time was ticking away. Mallory, Kyle, and Carolyn wanted to make it to a seven o'clock movie. But it didn't look like that was going to happen. It was six-thirty already, and still no sign of Renee.

Joanna had made it perfectly clear that she didn't want Mallory to leave without Renee. But Mallory didn't have to be told. Mallory wasn't about to do anything that might be construed by Renee as some kind of slight. In fact, Mallory had decided to go on an all-out campaign to befriend Renee. Too bad it wasn't working out very well.

The day had started with Renee snubbing Mallory once again. Mallory couldn't help feeling a little hurt that Renee had rejected the offer to go shopping with her. At the same time, she couldn't help feeling a little relieved to have some time off.

Having had a couple of hours to herself, Mallory was ready to face Renee, ready to try again. But she wasn't quite ready to do it without help. So Mallory asked Carolyn to go to the movies with her and Renee, to act as a buffer between them. She also asked Kyle.

It was a clever plan. Mallory wouldn't have to be alone with Renee, and she could set up Kyle and Carolyn at the same time. But thanks to Renee, that didn't seem to be working out either.

Mallory was determined that the evening not be a total waste. At least half her plan could still work out, the most important half as far as she was concerned.

"Why don't you guys go ahead to the movies," she suggested to Kyle and Carolyn. She shot Kyle a look that said it wasn't a suggestion at all, but an order.

"I don't know, Mal," Kyle said, obviously too afraid to commit himself either way.

"No way," Carolyn told her, leaning back into the couch to make it clear that she was staying put.

"Really," Mallory pushed it. "I don't mind. After all, there's no reason for all of us to sit around here doing nothing. That's stupid."

"We're not leaving you here all alone," Carolyn told her.

Just then the front door opened.

"Hello," Renee's voice called out.

"We're in the den, Renee," Mallory called back, trying to keep the frustration out of her voice.

Renee came into the room laden with packages and apologies. Joanna came out of the kitchen to greet her.

"Let's see what you got," Joanna said without even asking about why Renee was so late.

As Renee complied, Joanna oohed and aahed and complimented Renee on her good taste. Mallory, Carolyn, and Kyle agreed that Renee had bought some really nice things. Renee seemed pleased with their opinions.

Mallory didn't want to appear rude by rushing Renee, but there was still time to catch the movie—if they left immediately.

"We were headed out to see a movie and maybe get something to eat afterward," Mallory spoke up. "We were hoping that you would come along."

"Oh, I couldn't," Renee declined.

She did it nicely, but Mallory couldn't help feeling that Renee had just blown her off again.

"I really would like to join you," Renee went on. "But I'm way too tired. It's been a long day. You all go ahead though. Don't let me ruin your fun."

Mallory didn't know what to say. She was afraid to say anything, because she knew that anything she said would be wrong.

Fortunately, Carolyn picked up the slack for her. "Why don't we all just stay here and rent some movies," she suggested.

"Actually, I think I'm just going to go up to bed," Renee answered. "I really am that tired. So please don't make your plans around me."

"Well, what do you want to do?" Kyle asked tentatively.

"Go to the movies, I guess," Mallory answered.

Just then the telephone rang. Mallory reached for it.

"Hello," she said into the receiver.

"Hi, girlie," the voice on the other end greeted her. "It's Trudy." As if Mallory didn't know that. "May I speak with your mother, please?"

Mallory handed the phone over to Joanna, who gestured for Mallory to wait for a second before running out the door. By the time Joanna hung up, she wasn't very happy.

"Dee Ann never showed up for work tonight," Joanna told them, sounding more disappointed than angry. "Trudy offered to cover, but I told her absolutely not. That woman only takes off one day a week as it is. I was hoping that one of you girls would be willing to cover the shift," she said to Carolyn and Mallory.

"No problem," Carolyn beat Mallory to it. "I'll be happy to go in."

"You haven't had a day off all week either," Mallory told Carolyn. "I'll go in. You and Kyle go to the movies."

It was the perfect solution. That way Kyle and Carolyn would go on a real date, even if they didn't know that's what it was.

"That does sound like the best idea," Joanna

decided. "Thanks, Mal. You're a good daughter."
Joanna put her arm around her daughter and gave
her a quick squeeze.

Mallory saw Renee flinch, as if she'd been hit.
It was the first time that Mallory had ever seen a
chink in Renee's armor. And in that instant,
Mallory understood what it was all about between
her and Renee. It was a battle over Joanna.
Mallory couldn't help feeling sorry for Renee.
Because she knew that it was a battle Renee could
never win.

CHAPTER

14

"Oh, miss," the obnoxious woman at table twelve bellowed. "We're still waiting for our check."

Mallory forced an accommodating smile as she struggled to balance the tray of food she was trying to get to table four. "I'll be with you in just a second."

The woman huffed as she reached across the table to take yet another forkful of the pie her husband hadn't finished.

The restaurant was packed, and Mallory was having a difficult time trying to stay on top of all her tables. It wasn't that Mallory was a bad waitress. In fact, had there really been a Miss Congeniality contest, Mallory's tableside manners would have definitely positioned her as a top contender. It was just that Mallory hadn't had a whole lot of practice at waiting tables. Thanks to her mother's bleeding heart, Mallory was never put on a regular schedule in the restaurant. Joanna insisted that the waiter and waitressing shifts be given to the people who most needed the tips, so most of the time, Mallory worked as a cashier.

"Here you are, ma'am," Mallory said as she finally handed the obnoxious woman her check. "The desserts are on me," she told her. "Thanks for being so patient."

The obnoxious woman smiled her gratitude before she swallowed up the last crumb on her husband's plate.

Just then the bell in the kitchen summoned Mallory, signaling that her next order was ready to go out. But as Mallory headed toward the swinging doors, Dee Ann burst through them, carrying Mallory's order.

"Just leave me your open checks," Dee Ann said as she blew past Mallory, "and you can get out of here." Dee Ann headed for Mallory's table. The one that was bound to leave a ten-dollar tip.

"Oh, I don't think so," Mallory told her as she followed Dee Ann back into the kitchen.

"This is my shift," Dee Ann informed her, without even turning around.

"Yeah," Mallory said. "But you never showed up for it. So now it's my shift."

"Get lost," Dee Ann shot back.

"You can't just walk in here two hours late and expect to take over like you've been here the entire time!" Mallory was fuming.

"Oh, yeah?" Dee Ann shot back as she spun around and grabbed the rest of Mallory's checks from Mallory's apron. "Just watch me." Dee Ann started to walk away.

Mallory couldn't believe Dee Ann's nerve. Not only had Dee Ann shown up two hours late without offering any explanation or apology, much less any gratitude to Mallory for covering for her, she looked like she'd been through a war. Even Joanna wouldn't be too thrilled with the idea of Dee Ann greeting customers in the state she was in. Dee Ann's uniform looked as though it hadn't been washed or ironed in days. And her spiked hairdo was less spiked than matted. But as Mallory grabbed Dee Ann's arm to stop her, she caught the most disturbing sight of all.

The side of Dee Ann's face was puffy and bruised. Mallory could see the black-and-blue marks shining through the two inches of make-up Dee Ann had caked on. And the purple lipstick Dee Ann was wearing did nothing more than highlight the fact that her lip was split and swollen.

Mallory gasped. "What happened to you?"

Dee Ann's eyes flashed with hostility. "I don't have to answer to you," she shot back.

"Dee Ann," Mallory tried again. "Your face looks awful. What happened?"

"None of your business," Dee Ann said as she pulled away from Mallory's grip. "Touch me again," she added, "and it's your own face you'll have to worry about."

Fine, Mallory thought as anger surged through her again. If Dee Ann wanted to exchange threats, then that's exactly what she'd do. "My mother and Trudy know that you didn't show up tonight, Dee Ann," Mallory said through clenched teeth. "That's why I'm here."

Dee Ann laughed. "Yeah, well, now I did show up. And now *you* can go home."

Mallory whirled around without saying another word.

"Where do you think you're going?" Dee Ann demanded, following her.

"I'm calling my mother," Mallory told her. "You can't pull this stunt."

Dee Ann laughed. "I already have."

Mallory turned back to look at Dee Ann.

"I already called your mommy," Dee Ann informed her. "And she told me to tell you to go home now."

Mallory wasn't buying it. "Yeah, right."

"She did," Dee Ann insisted. "If you want, you can call her yourself and ask her."

"My mother had no problems at all with your showing up two hours late without calling anyone to fill in for you?" Mallory asked.

"Nope. No problem at all once I explained about how I fell down the cellar steps helping my boyfriend's mother with the laundry," Dee Ann told her. "And she was really understanding when

I told her I couldn't have called from home. The phone company turned off the phone because I didn't have enough money to pay last month's bill."

Suddenly Mallory didn't know who she hated more, herself or Dee Ann.

"That's when she told me that she would explain it all to Trudy, and that I should send you home," Dee Ann said with a smirk.

"Fine," Mallory huffed. "But you know, Dee Ann," she went on, "you could have just told me the truth. And you could have at least thanked me for filling in."

Dee Ann glared at Mallory. "You want me to kiss your precious little feet or something?"

Mallory shook her head in disgust as she turned to walk away.

"Hey, Mal," Dee Ann called after her. "I didn't fall down the steps. I took a fist to my face trying to strangle someone who irritates me a whole lot less than you do."

Mallory didn't even bother turning around to the sound of Dee Ann's malicious laughter.

CHAPTER 15

"I had a really great time tonight," Kyle said to Carolyn as he threw the car into park. They were in front of Mallory's house, where Carolyn had left her car before she and Kyle went out to the movies. Kyle left the car running and the radio on, hoping to spend a little more time with Carolyn alone. "Thanks for coming out with me."

"You can thank Mallory for that." Carolyn laughed.

Kyle laughed too. "Yeah. She did a really good job setting us up, didn't she?"

"I can't help feeling a little guilty about it though," Carolyn said. "You and I had such a great time, while poor Mallory had to go to work for Dee Ann. She isn't even home yet."

Kyle noticed that Mallory's car wasn't in the driveway. "Trust me," he said, trying to get over his own feelings of guilt. "Mallory is probably much happier at work than she would be sitting at home with Renee."

"She and Renee aren't doing well together, are they?" Carolyn commented.

"No, they're not," Kyle told her. "And I have to tell you, it's really Renee's fault. No matter how hard Mallory tries to be friendly, Renee makes it perfectly clear that she wants Mallory to leave her alone. I just don't get it. Mallory is the easiest person on earth to get along with. I mean, look at the two of you. You guys hit it off right away."

Carolyn nodded her agreement. "Maybe Renee is just having a tough time being away from home," she suggested. "I know I am."

"Really?" Kyle asked, happy to be able to change the subject from Renee to something much more interesting, and much more pleasant—Carolyn. "You don't like being away from home?"

"Not one bit," she answered. "In fact, it really stinks. You'd be surprised at all the things you miss. Silly little things. Things you never even think about until you don't have them anymore."

"Don't you like the people you're living with?" Kyle asked.

"It's not that," Carolyn answered. "I just don't like being away from home."

"Would you rather be living in a dorm?"

"No," Carolyn answered. "I like privacy. Besides, if I lived in a dorm, who knows how much work I'd actually get done."

Carolyn seemed far away all of a sudden, lost in her own thoughts.

"I hope you're not sorry you came here," he said, trying to snap her out of it.

It worked. Carolyn smiled at him, the same way she'd been smiling at him all evening. "No," she told him, "I'm not sorry at all. In fact, things are working out a lot better than I thought they would. In just a few weeks I've found a great job and made great friends, and I really am looking forward to college."

"What are you going to study?" Kyle asked, suddenly aware of how little he really knew about Carolyn. That seemed odd, especially after he'd spent the entire evening feeling as though he'd known her all his life.

"Well, the first year all you do is take required courses," she explained. "You don't really declare a major until your junior year. But I think I'll probably go for a degree in teaching. That's why I decided to come here. Rydner is one of the best schools for that. At least one of the best I could afford."

"A teacher, huh?" Kyle considered that for a moment. "I can see that," he decided. "You're a natural with kids. You're always so good with them in the deli, and they really seem to like you a lot. You'd probably be a great teacher."

"Thanks." Carolyn smiled at the compliment. "But I'm not sure I'll end up teaching. Maybe I'll be a guidance counselor, or even a child psychologist.

I know I want to work with children, but beyond that, I'm not sure. How about you? Do you know what you want to do when you get out of school?"

"I just hope I do get out of school someday." Kyle laughed. "After that, who knows. I'll probably end up working for my father."

"That's nice," she said.

"I suppose." Kyle shrugged. "It's safe anyway. Safe and comfortable. That's the story of my life. Safe and comfortable."

"You sound like you're complaining," she chided him.

"I know I shouldn't," he said, meaning it. "But sometimes it just feels so boring."

"There are people who would kill to have the life you've got," Carolyn told him. "Most people don't have it nearly as good. Take Renee for instance."

"Oh, no." He stopped her. "The last thing I want to talk about is Renee. It's all I ever talk about with Mallory anymore."

"Okay," she agreed. "No more talk about Renee. What should we talk about then?"

Kyle was happy that she was in no hurry to get out of the car. That was a good sign. He tried to hold his enthusiasm in check. One date did not make a relationship. But Kyle couldn't help thinking that they were off to a pretty good start. He'd never had such a good first date. And he had never dated anyone as smart as Carolyn, or as nice, or as pretty. He wanted to know everything there was to know about Carolyn Michaels. "You," he answered. "I want to talk about you."

"All right." She laughed. "What do you want to know?"

What he really wanted to know was how Carolyn felt about him. But that wasn't a question he could ask. He had to come up with another question. And he was having trouble doing it. "I don't know," he said. "Tell me about your family. Like, do you have any brothers or sisters?" Kyle couldn't believe he'd asked such a dumb question. But it was the only thing he could think of.

Carolyn didn't act as though it was dumb at all. "I have a brother," she answered. "He's younger than I am, and he still lives at home."

"Are you close to him?" Kyle asked.

"Close enough to hate his little guts," she answered with a chuckle. "You don't know how lucky you are to be an only child."

"I never really felt like I needed a brother or a sister," Kyle told her. "Maybe it's because I've always had Mallory. And that was better than having a sister because she didn't live in my house."

"Yeah, when they live in your house, it's a real nightmare," she said, only half-kidding. "You spend all your time trying to think of ways to get rid of them."

"Do you think you would have been happier with a sister?" Kyle asked.

"No," Carolyn answered. "I hear that's much worse."

"I guess I'm lucky to have escaped the sibling rivalry thing," Kyle joked.

"They say you grow out of it," Carolyn said. "But I'm not holding my breath."

"Okay. So you hate your brother," Kyle teased. "What about your parents?"

Carolyn didn't answer. She had that faraway look in her eye again.

"Carolyn?" he nudged her.

"Shhh," she ordered.

"What's wrong?" he asked.

Carolyn didn't answer. She just reached out to turn up the volume on the radio.

It was a news report. "Maribeth Riley is eight and a half years old," the newscaster's voice said over the air. "She has blond hair and blue eyes. She is three feet nine inches tall and weighs sixty-eight pounds. She was last seen by her mother shortly after two o'clock this afternoon. At that time she was wearing pink shorts and a matching T-shirt. If anybody has seen this child, please call the police department immediately."

Carolyn turned off the radio and shook her head sadly.

"Wow," Kyle reacted to the report. "Another

little kid missing. That's terrible."

"Yeah," Carolyn agreed. "It makes you realize just how fragile 'safe and comfortable' really is."

Kyle looked at Carolyn and saw tears glistening in her eyes. He couldn't help being touched by how sweet and sensitive she was. His instinct was to put his arm around her, to comfort her. But he stopped himself. He didn't want his gesture to be construed as a come-on. So he did nothing. Nor could he think of anything to say.

The moment of silence was broken by the sound of a car horn. It was with relief that Kyle recognized Mallory's car as it pulled past them and into the driveway. When he looked at Carolyn again, she was smiling.

"What do you think we should tell her about our date?" Carolyn asked.

Kyle was happy to hear her refer to their evening together as a date. "Well, under normal circumstances I would say that we should tell her what a lousy time we had. Really goof on her. Just to make her sweat. But with all she's been going through, I don't think she'd appreciate the joke."

"I think you're right," Carolyn agreed. "I think we ought to tell her the truth. The whole, happy truth." She reached out and squeezed his hand. Just for a second. Then she opened her door and got out of the car.

For a moment, Kyle was too stunned to move.

Too stunned and too happy. By the time he did get out of the car, Mallory was already on her way down the driveway to meet them. He could see that she was already smiling, already anticipating the good news. That was exactly what she was going to hear. Nothing but good news.

For the time being, the missing children were forgotten.

CHAPTER 16

"Hey, Trudy!"

Trudy Zigler smiled and waved at the little girl jumping rope in the driveway next to her own as she pulled the deli van toward the closed garage doors at the end of her drive.

"Hey, girlie," Trudy said as she stepped out of the van, carrying the lockbox containing her gun and a couple of newspapers folded under her arm. "How's my favorite neighbor?"

The little girl smiled. "Good."

"Isn't it getting kind of late to be outside all by yourself?" Trudy asked.

"Nah," the little girl answered. "There's still some light out. And my mommy said it was okay as long as I stayed in the driveway where she could see me."

Trudy smiled. "Yeah, well, you make sure you do just that."

"I know." The little girl rolled her eyes as if she'd been given the same instructions a thousand times.

"I know you know." Trudy laughed as she

headed toward her front steps. But Trudy Zigler couldn't help thinking how easy it was to con a child into forgetting what he or she had been taught. Yeah. Little children were so easily distracted, so easily swayed. As Trudy stole one last glance at the girl, she was quite certain that with the right kind of enticement, even her "favorite neighbor" would skip right down the driveway and out of her mommy's sight forever.

But that wasn't going to happen. Not with Trudy living right next door.

Trudy closed the door behind her and dropped the lockbox on the table by the front closet. She opened the closet door and pulled out a stack of scrapbooks that was buried under a pile of jackets. Then she headed into the tiny kitchen with the newspapers still tucked under her arm. The newspapers that reported the disappearance of Jack Riley's little girl . . . last seen playing in her own driveway.

Trudy set the scrapbooks down on the kitchen table, eager to cut out the articles about Jack Riley's daughter. She wanted to paste them inside her newest scrapbook, the one that contained all the articles about Dr. Baxter's missing child and the flyer that was still being handed out at the deli. The flyer that wasn't "doing squat." In more than two weeks' time, not a soul had stepped forward with information about Dr. Baxter's little girl. And

Trudy Zigler was willing to bet her life that no one would. Once the hours turned into days, and the days into weeks, it was a pretty safe bet that the only place the weeks would lead was to months and months of futile searching, guaranteed to lessen in intensity with the passage of time.

Trudy unfolded *The Gazette*, the Pennsylvania paper she had crossed state lines to get. In fact, Trudy picked up *The Gazette* in a fancy neighborhood convenience store not two miles from Jack Riley's house. It was a local township paper that no out-of-state store carried, including the deli. There was no reason to. Township papers generally reported just township news. Which was why Trudy wanted to get her hands on this one. The disappearance of Jack Riley's little girl was the biggest news Jack Riley's posh Pennsylvania township had ever experienced. Trudy just couldn't resist getting a look at what kind of "wonderful" things Jack Riley's local paper would have to say about him now.

"Hmmm, hmmm, hmmm . . ." Trudy shook her head as she sat staring at the picture on the front page. The picture of Jack Riley and his wife, holding what appeared to be a press conference right in their perfectly landscaped front yard. "You're not looking too good here, Jack," Trudy mused. "What's the matter?" she asked the picture as if it were Jack Riley himself. "Being the prosecuted doesn't feel so good, huh?" Trudy sighed. "No. Being the prosecuted feels a whole lot different from being a 'brilliant prosecutor,' doesn't it, Jack?"

Trudy reached for the scrapbook she had labeled "Baby D." It wasn't a new scrapbook. In fact, it was one of the oldest scrapbooks Trudy had. She had planned to paste the articles about Dr. Elaine Baxter's little girl in her "Baby D" scrapbook, but there weren't any pages left, so Trudy went out and bought a new one. She'd labeled it "Baby D, Two." It was already starting to fill up.

Trudy flipped through the original "Baby D" scrapbook, until she landed on another front page picture of Jack Riley, the first "news" photo ever taken of the then "unknown" attorney. As Trudy looked at the picture of Jack Riley, smiling for the cameras as he climbed the courthouse steps, positioned right behind Lorene and Calvin Burnell, Trudy wanted to puke. Yeah. Jack Riley knew beyond a shadow of a doubt that those courthouse steps would catapult him right to the top of the ladder. And Jack Riley was right. Only Jack Riley wasn't smiling anymore.

"You're definitely looking a whole lot happier here, Jack," Trudy said as she compared the pictures side by side. "Not to mention a heck of a lot younger."

Trudy flipped to another picture of Jack Riley in

her old "Baby D" scrapbook. The picture that was taken in the courtroom, the moment the final decision was handed down. "TRIUMPH OR TRAGEDY?" That's what the headline read. And while "triumph" was written all over Jack Riley's face, with Lorene and Calvin Burnell by his side jumping up like they'd just won a million-dollar lottery, behind Jack Riley were the faces that reflected what the decision really was.

Trudy's heart ached as she stared at the devastated images of Ryan Dunne struggling to keep Joanna Dunne on her feet, while C. J. and Michael Stoddard stood sobbing beside her. "Tragedy" didn't even begin to describe the decision that was handed down . . . or the events that followed.

Trudy could barely force herself to turn the page. She knew exactly what horrible moment the cameras had captured next. Just the thought of it was enough to traumatize Trudy, even now. Even with the safety of knowing that her "real" mommy and daddy were long dead, and despite the passage of so many years, Trudy Zigler was still haunted by that moment. She'd played it over and over again inside her head a thousand different times and a thousand different ways. But Trudy Zigler still couldn't handle the idea that one horrible moment was all it really took to destroy an innocent life.

"BABY D IS GOING HOME."

Trudy could barely read the headline through the tears that were welling up in her eyes. As she forced herself to look down at the photo of Baby D screaming for her mommy, clinging desperately to the life that sustained her, Trudy Zigler started to cry. The image of Dr. Elaine Baxter ripping Baby D from her mommy's arms, with Baby D's little fist wrapped tightly around the one thing the vultures couldn't seem to pry free from her hands—the locket on her mommy's necklace—was a traumatizing sight. One that was sure to haunt Trudy Zigler until the day she died.

Trudy was starting to lose it. She could feel it happening. If she didn't do something soon, she was going to fall victim to one of her "little spells."

Trudy got up from the table, trembling like a leaf as her heart began to race and her head started reeling. She felt light-headed and dizzy again, and it was less than forty-eight hours since her last spell. Trudy Zigler's one day off hardly provided her with the rest that she needed—even though she had spent the majority of it unconscious.

Trudy opened the refrigerator and pulled out the rest of the apple pie. She needed something sweet. Somehow, that always seemed to help, even though the doctors had assured her that blood sugar wasn't a concern.

As Trudy took a fork to the pie, eating more than she really wanted to, she started to feel better. In no time at all, she was back at the table, working on her new scrapbook.

Trudy started to paste the *Gazette* article into her scrapbook, right after the page with the pink flyer. Then her mind wandered back to the day the decision came down. It was a date that was burned into her broken heart forever. And it was a date that was creeping up again. Yeah. In just a couple of weeks, September twenty-first would be back to haunt her.

And Trudy Zigler had the funny feeling that she was going to need another scrapbook.

CHAPTER 17

"No wonder you're always shootin' your mouth off about this place," Arthur Ditmars said as Dee Ann climbed off the back of his Harley. "Last time I seen a house like this was on that show about lifestyles of the rich and famous."

"Yeah," Dee Ann told her boyfriend. "Well, do me a favor and don't act like you're all impressed or anything in front of these people, okay? Just pretend that you've been to lots of places even nicer than this one. And try to act like you fit in. I don't want you embarrassing me in front of Joanna."

"You ain't gotta worry about me, darlin'." Arthur Ditmars spit out the wad of chewing tobacco he had in his mouth as he shut down the roaring engine of his Harley and threw down the kickstand. "Don't I always act like a perfect gentleman?" He grabbed Dee Ann's arm and pulled her toward him. "Although you seem to like it a whole lot when I don't."

"Cut it out, Snake," Dee Ann insisted as she fought off Arthur Ditmars's roaming hands.

"Snake" wasn't a pet name Dee Ann used for

her boyfriend. "Snake" was the name he'd won the day he passed his initiation into the Desperados, one of the most notorious biker organizations on the East Coast.

While Arthur Ditmars claimed that the Desperados were simply a bunch of guys with motorcycles who decided to form a little club, the Desperados were exactly what their "club" name suggested. And Arthur Ditmars had passed his initiation with flying colors. Yeah. Arthur Ditmars could wreak havoc with the best of them, slipping away from the law the same way he slipped up on his victims—like a "snake in the grass."

It had been years since Arthur Ditmars's initiation day. In fact, Arthur Ditmars was on his way to becoming president of one of the Desperados' state chapters. It was a title bestowed on only the best of the best, the guys whose qualifications were unsurpassed. The guys who made simple assault look like a camping game for Boy Scouts. "President" was a hard-won title. And Arthur "the Snake" Ditmars would kill for it.

"What's the matter, sugar?" Snake asked Dee Ann, behaving more like an octopus wrapping its long tentacles around its prey. "You already embarrassed by me?"

"No," Dee Ann lied as she tried to wriggle her way out of his grip. "Somebody might see us, that's all."

"So what?" Snake hissed venomously. "You don't want me touchin' you in front of these people either?"

Snake's grip suddenly felt threatening. Dee Ann's entire body went rigid, knowing full well that if she answered that question honestly, she'd be in for another war, right in front of Joanna Dunne's house. Dee Ann was not about to let that happen.

"You know I love it when you touch me," Dee Ann said, forcing herself to smile coyly as she tried to defuse the situation. "It's just that they think I'm, like, 'Miss Goody Two-Shoes,'" she said, cracking her gum. "That's all. And I don't want to blow the image."

Snake laughed as he finally released his hold on her. "Blind *and* rich," he said, climbing off his Harley. "Now that's what I call a winning combination." Snake winked at Dee Ann. "Something tells me I'm gonna like these people a whole lot." Snake reached down to grab Dee Ann's hand. Then he stopped himself, throwing his hands up in the air as if someone had just pulled a gun on him. "It's okay if I hold your hand, isn't it?" Snake teased. "I mean even 'good girls' are allowed to hold hands, aren't they?"

Dee Ann rolled her eyes. She wanted to tell Snake that it wasn't okay, that she didn't want him holding her hand in front of Joanna, but she couldn't. Dee Ann wasn't about to push her luck with Snake any further than she already had. "You're such a jerk." Dee Ann was careful to deliver that news playfully.

"So which way to the shindig?" Snake asked as he grabbed hold of her hand and started past the string of cars lining the block in front of both Joanna's and C. J.'s houses.

"It's a picnic," Dee Ann corrected him. "Not a shindig."

"Oh, no, darlin'," Snake informed her. "Now that we're here, it's definitely gonna be a shindig."

That was exactly what Dee Ann was trying to avoid. She hadn't wanted to bring Snake to Joanna and C. J.'s Labor Day picnic at all, but Snake had insisted. And Snake was pretty persuasive when he wanted to be.

It wasn't that Dee Ann didn't want to include Snake in her life. She did. In fact, Snake was the only person from her past she'd held on to. She'd met him around the time she'd decided to get rid of her parents and leave home. And she'd decided to do that long before she figured out how. Dee Ann was all of thirteen years old when Snake entered her life, and it was Snake who had helped her get out of it.

Snake was nearly eleven years older than Dee Ann, and from the moment he blew into town, he was totally taken with her. While he'd insisted that he was just "passing through," he "passed through" a lot, just to see Dee Ann. And Dee Ann lived to see Snake.

On top of being the only person who seemed to understand her, Snake provided the kind of attention that Dee Ann felt starved for—at least in the beginning. Snake was always there with a shoulder to cry on, with no strings attached. And while Dee Ann had sometimes imagined herself in someone else's arms, she was always grateful for his being there, for having someone bigger and stronger to hold on to. So when Snake finally offered her a way out of the life that was making her so miserable, Dee Ann had jumped at it. Thanks to Snake, Dee Ann had somewhere to go. Only these days, there seemed to be lots of strings attached.

As Dee Ann headed down the street, holding the hand that had reached out to her when she most needed it, she couldn't help feeling a little bit guilty for being embarrassed by Snake. She really did love him. And he was going to be a part of the life she was trying to put together, as long as he didn't screw it up.

"I guess we can just walk across the lawn between the two houses and go straight into the back," Dee Ann told Snake. "The two yards together are like a park back there. Wait till you see it. It's beautiful."

Snake yanked Dee Ann back from taking another step. "I want to check out the house first," he told her as he started up Joanna Dunne's driveway.

Not two minutes into the thing, and Snake was already screwing up. "The picnic is in the yard." Dee Ann tugged back. "That's why they call it a picnic."

"Oh, come on, sugar." Snake pulled even harder. "I'm dying to see what your dream house looks like on the inside." He smiled at Dee Ann. "So I know exactly what I'm in for."

CHAPTER

18

Mallory couldn't believe that the summer was over already. There were still two more days until school started, but somehow those two days didn't count. As far as Mallory was concerned, Labor Day was it. So she was determined to make the most of it. And apparently, so was everybody else.

The backyard was full of people, all of them seeming to have a wonderful time. There were badminton and volleyball games. There were people chatting with their friends or just lazing in the sun. Nobody had been in the pool yet, but as the day wore on, that would change. Sooner or later someone would get up the courage to be the first one in. Or Kyle would end up pushing someone in, just to get the ball rolling.

It was a terrific picnic, especially judging by the amount of food people were consuming. Mallory found it both amazing and amusing that people who worked around food all day could scarf down hot dogs, burgers, and salads with such abandon. They were already halfway through the third bowl of her mother's homemade potato salad. But then, maybe that was the answer. Joanna and C. J. had prepared all the food themselves. And their employees really seemed to appreciate it.

It was an appropriate Labor Day celebration. The bosses catered to their workers, treating them to a day of fun and relaxation. None of the employees was allowed to lift a finger. All the work was done by the Dunnes and the Stoddards.

Mallory made her way over to her father and Michael Stoddard, who had both been assigned grill duty.

"What can I get you, Mal?" Ryan Dunne asked, obviously enjoying his role of cook for the day.

"Nothin'," she answered. "I just came over to see how you were doing."

"We haven't burned anything yet." Michael Stoddard gave her a wink.

"In fact," Ryan Dunne proclaimed proudly, "we've been getting nothing but compliments on our cooking."

Mallory laughed. Flipping stuff on the grill didn't exactly qualify these two as "Galloping Gourmets," but it was as close as they were going to get. "Everybody seems to be having a good time," she said. "I think this picnic is a really nice idea."

"I'll second that," said Trudy, who was suddenly beside them.

"Are you having a good time, Trudy?" Ryan Dunne asked her.

"Sure am," Trudy told him. "Everyone is."

"Glad to hear it." Ryan turned his attention back to his daughter. "Hey, Mal, would you mind tending the grill for a second so Michael and I can grab a cold drink and take a short breather?"

"Sure, Dad," Mallory answered.

"You don't have to trouble yourself with that, girlie. I'll be happy to take over," Trudy offered, trying to intercept the barbecue fork as Ryan passed it to Mallory.

"Oh, no, you don't," Michael Stoddard chided good-naturedly. "If our wives see you flipping those burgers, they'll have both our heads."

"You know the rules, Trudy," Ryan Dunne reminded her. "No work for you. You just have fun and relax." He handed the fork over to Mallory, winked at Trudy, and then he and Michael Stoddard headed for the cooler for something to drink.

"But this *is* how I relax," Trudy protested.

"Not today," Mallory told her authoritatively, getting a kick out of being able to boss Trudy around for once. "You heard my dad; go have some fun."

Trudy smiled at Mallory and nodded. But the

expression on her face made her look like a foreign traveler who didn't understand the language. Her eyes scanned the yard, looking for something to do, someplace to go. And as luck would have it, Trudy managed to find a situation that needed her attention.

The volleyball game had been getting increasingly boisterous. When the ball flew out of bounds and bounced off the food table, Trudy decided that it was time to put the kibosh on it.

"Take it easy over there," Trudy shouted at the players. "One more wild ball, and I'm gonna shut that game down." Then she headed over to the food table to make sure no damage was done.

Trudy was back on patrol, the self-appointed picnic police. All she needed was a uniform. But Trudy was able to keep law and order even in her picnic outfit.

Now there was a sight to behold, Mallory thought. Trudy's picnic outfit looked a lot like the costume that Mallory had worn in the school production of Oklahoma! Only Mallory's prairie dress was green. Trudy's was pink.

"Hey, Mal," a voice hollered, taking Mallory's attention away from Trudy.

Mallory turned just in time to see the water balloon sailing toward her. Instinctively, her hand shot out in front of her. It was too late to catch the balloon gently and prevent it from exploding, but at least she managed to keep the explosion far enough away from her body so that she didn't get drenched. Not that it mattered. She had her bathing suit on anyway, under a pair of shorts. After all, water balloon attacks were par for the course at a picnic.

"Missed me!" Mallory taunted her assailant. Then it registered that it was Renee. For a moment, Mallory felt upset. Had it been anybody else who'd thrown the water balloon, Mallory would have accepted it as harmless fun. But because it came from Renee, she had to wonder if the gesture had a malicious edge.

Renee's laughter told her that it really was only harmless fun. Her laughter was innocent, the laughter of a child at play.

Mallory's smile returned. It grew even wider when she realized that Renee had called her "Mal"—just like one of her friends. She didn't know if this sense of camaraderie would last beyond the picnic, but she was going to enjoy it for as long as it did last. Maybe she could even begin to make some headway with Renee.

"You're gonna pay for that," Mallory threatened playfully.

"You'll have to catch me first," Renee shot back. Then she was off to find a victim for the water balloon she still had in her other hand.

"Count on it," Mallory called after her, as if

Renee were any other friend.

It was the first time that Mallory had felt truly at ease with Renee. And as she stood there smiling to herself, she couldn't help thinking that maybe everything was starting to go right.

CHAPTER 19

"**W**hat in the world is that?" C. J. gasped.
Joanna knew exactly what it was that had caught C. J.'s attention, because she was transfixed by the sight herself. "That must be Dee Ann's boyfriend," Joanna answered numbly, hoping that she was wrong.

"That guy looks old enough to be her father," C. J. said, sounding every bit as appalled as Joanna felt. "I thought you said Dee Ann and the boyfriend lived with his mother?"

"That's what she told me," Joanna replied. It was obvious that she and C. J. had jumped to the wrong conclusion on the basis of that information. They had assumed that because the boyfriend still lived with his mother, he was probably the same age as Dee Ann, or at least in the same generation.

"Looking at him, that's hard to believe," C. J. said through clenched teeth and a wide, fake smile.

Joanna put on her most polite smile, too, as Dee Ann approached them with the boyfriend in tow. Joanna didn't want to smile. What she really wanted to do was grab that kid by the scruff of the neck and ask her what the hell she was doing with her life. But it wasn't her place to do that. After all, she was not Dee Ann's mother.

"Hi, Mom." Dee Ann greeted Joanna the same way she always did. "Hi, C. J.," she added just as brightly.

"Hello, Dee Ann," the women said, practically in unison.

"I was beginning to think you might not come," Joanna added.

"My fault we're late," the boyfriend apologized. "I had some business to take care of this morning."

As Joanna wondered what kind of "business," Dee Ann made introductions.

"Joanna, C. J., this is my boyfriend, Arthur Ditmars."

"Pleased to meetcha." He stuck out his hand.

"Nice meeting you," Joanna lied, offering her hand. She tried not to flinch when he just about crushed her knuckles in the shake.

C. J. was not so demure about it. "That's quite a grip you've got there, Arthur," she said, rubbing her hand once he'd released it.

He didn't apologize. "My friends call me Snake," he told them.

Joanna smiled politely as C. J. shot her a look.

"Nice place you got here," he commented.

"Thank you." Joanna accepted the compliment graciously. But it didn't feel quite so much a compliment as it did a threat.

Snake's eyes never stopped moving. It was as if he was casing the joint. Even Joanna, who made all kinds of allowances for people, couldn't convince herself that Snake was harmless. It didn't take a lot of street smarts to understand that Snake was every bit as dangerous as the king cobra he had tattooed around his forearm.

"So what do you do, Arthur?" C. J. asked.

"I'm sort of between jobs right now," he answered.

"I see," C. J. said. "Well, what *did* you do?"

"This and that." He smirked.

Joanna could see Dee Ann squirm in the uncomfortable silence that followed.

"Why don't you two help yourselves to something to eat," Joanna said, offering Dee Ann an easy out. "There's plenty of food."

"Yeah, and I notice you got a keg too," Snake said. "Mind if I help myself to a cold one?"

"That's what it's there for," Joanna answered, relieved at the opportunity to get away from Snake.

"Thanks," he said, grabbing Dee Ann's hand and heading for the keg. "Catch ya later," he shot back over his shoulder.

"Watch where you're going," Dee Ann

shrieked at Snake. She pulled him out of the way just in time to avoid a collision with a toddler who was making her way toward Joanna and C. J.

The little one seemed undaunted by the near miss until Snake squatted down to try and make friends.

"Aren't you a pretty little thing," he said, reaching out to tickle her under the chin.

The little girl let out a squeal of alarm, then turned and ran right into C. J.'s legs. C. J. bent down and scooped the baby up into her arms protectively.

"That's Alyssa," Dee Ann told Snake. "Dennis's little girl. I told you about Dennis. He runs the kitchen."

"Cute kid," Snake commented. "I love kids."

"Sure he does," Joanna whispered to C. J. as Snake and Dee Ann continued on their way.

"Only if they're properly cooked," C. J. whispered back, holding on to little Alyssa as if she'd just saved the child's life.

Dennis passed Dee Ann and Snake in his pursuit of his daughter, stopping just long enough for a quick introduction.

"That is one scary guy," Dennis said when he reached Joanna and C. J. Dennis was an ex-marine. Joanna knew it took a lot to unnerve him. "I just wonder if Dee Ann knows what she's into," he said, shaking his head sadly.

"She's not a bad girl." Joanna defended Dee Ann. There was something about Dee Ann that tugged at Joanna's heart.

"She's not a good girl either," Dennis warned, not for the first time.

C. J. nodded her agreement. Everybody was always warning Joanna to be careful when it came to Dee Ann.

"I look at that kid, and it's like my worst nightmare come true," Dennis continued. "All I can think of is I don't want my little girl to turn out like that."

"Not a chance," C. J. assured him. "With parents like you and Amy, this kid's gonna be just fine. Aren't you, Lyss?" She winked at the little girl in her arms, who just giggled back and continued to play with C. J.'s earrings.

"I'd like to think so." Dennis smiled at the compliment. "But still, you worry. You've got to wonder whatever happened to a kid like Dee Ann to make her turn out the way she is."

Joanna wondered about that all the time.

CHAPTER 20

"It really is beautiful back here," Carolyn told Kyle as the two of them sat on the swings in the back of the yard, finishing off their burgers. "I never realized just how big this property really is."

"It just looks big," Kyle said, smiling awkwardly. "I mean, if you separated the two lots, it wouldn't really be all that impressive at all."

Immediately, Kyle wished he could take back the remark.

Carolyn's smile told Kyle that it had sounded just as stupid as he thought it did. Separated or not, the land behind the Dunnes' and the Stoddards' homes was incredibly impressive. And while Ryan Dunne and Michael Stoddard had designed the properties as if they were one, so that the two families shared everything, from an Olympic-sized swimming pool right down to the regulation-sized tennis courts, there was more than enough land to accommodate two sets of both, and then some.

Kyle wanted to kick himself. Why couldn't he just admit that his parents had tons of money instead of trying to deny it and coming off like a phony?

"You know," Carolyn teased him, "I really don't think any less of you because you have a great backyard."

"Oh, yeah?" Kyle laughed, letting his defenses drop. He should have known Carolyn wouldn't judge him based on one dumb remark. "And why is that?" he asked playfully.

Carolyn's grin was just as playful. "Because how could I possibly think any less of you than I already do? Great backyard or not," she added.

Kyle cracked up as he got up from his swing and pitched their empty plates into one of the trash bins that had been placed around the property. "I really set myself up for that one, didn't I?"

"Yup," Carolyn said, laughing, "you really did."

Kyle grabbed hold of the chains that were supporting Carolyn's swing and pulled her toward him. "So you don't think I'm just a privileged little weenie boy with nothing to offer but a great backyard, huh?"

Carolyn smiled as she moved her face closer to Kyle's. "Hardly," she said.

Carolyn's piercing blue eyes seemed to covet Kyle's very soul. And Kyle was so transfixed by them, so taken by Carolyn, that his heart was beating as wildly as a boy about to steal his first kiss.

He felt his skin getting hot and sweaty, and he was sure that his face was turning a bright shade of red.

Kiss the girl, you idiot!

But just as Kyle was about to do that, Carolyn started to turn away, looking a little embarrassed herself.

Kyle reached out gently to turn Carolyn's face back toward his own, refusing to let the moment he'd been waiting for pass him by. And as Carolyn smiled up at him sweetly, Kyle could tell that she was feeling just as awkward and nervous as he was.

The first kiss was always the hardest. Kyle wanted to get it over with so that they could move on to the second and third, which were always much more comfortable, and a whole lot easier to initiate.

But Kyle was wrong. He knew it the moment Carolyn's lips met his own. While the initiation part had been awkward, the kiss seemed so comfortable and familiar, Kyle felt as if he were sharing it with someone he'd been with his entire life.

And suddenly he was in no hurry to get it over with.

But he didn't really have a choice.

"So, I guess *you* guys are having a good time."

The sound of Joanna's voice sent Carolyn practically toppling backward off the swing. Kyle grabbed her arm to stop her from falling.

"A little too good." C. J. shot her son a look that managed to ice down the last bit of hot blood that was pulsating through his veins.

Joanna smiled her apology to both Carolyn and Kyle for aiding and abetting what seemed to be a surprise attack.

"Ew!" Dennis's little girl crinkled up her nose. "They were kissing," she told C. J., pointing her finger at Kyle and Carolyn.

C. J. laughed. "Pretty gross stuff, huh?"

Alyssa shook her head, cringing, as if the cootie bug itself was running loose in the yard.

"Have you met Dennis's little girl?" Joanna asked Carolyn, trying to make Carolyn feel a little less embarrassed than she looked.

"No." Carolyn smiled as she bent down to introduce herself. "I'm Carolyn," she said.

"And this is Alyssa," C. J. told her as the little girl suddenly turned shy.

"Hi, Alyssa," Carolyn said. "It's really nice to meet you."

Alyssa smiled. "I'm going on the airplane swing," she told Carolyn, pointing to the baby swing.

"You are?" Carolyn asked excitedly.

"Uh-huh," Alyssa answered.

"Wow," Carolyn said. "I wish I could go on the airplane swing."

"You're too big," Alyssa informed her,

sounding sorry for breaking the bad news.

"But you're not." Carolyn grinned as Alyssa's eyes grew wide with anticipation.

Kyle smiled. Carolyn was definitely a natural with kids.

"Okay, kiddo," Joanna said as she scooped Alyssa up. "You ready for take-off?"

Alyssa nodded as Joanna put her into the swing.

"Three . . . two . . . one," Alyssa yelled, excitedly. "Takeoff!" Her little legs started pumping furiously through the two leg holes in the bottom of the plane.

Joanna and C. J. cracked up.

"We've got to push you," Joanna told Alyssa as she stepped behind the swing.

"But first you've got to buckle up," C. J. said as she pulled the safety strap around Alyssa's waist.

"Kyle." Joanna was still laughing. "Go get Dennis and Amy," she told him. "They have to see this."

"I'll go find them," Carolyn told Kyle as she headed toward the center of the lawn.

Kyle went after her. "Hey," he said, grabbing her hand the second he caught up. "You don't think you can get rid of me that easily, do you?" he teased.

Carolyn immediately looked back at C. J. and pulled her hand from Kyle's grasp.

"It's okay," Kyle said as he took her hand again. "My mother's too busy playing with that baby to notice whether or not I'm holding your hand. And even if she was watching us," Kyle assured her, "it's still okay."

Carolyn didn't try to pull away, but she did start walking a whole lot faster.

Kyle couldn't help laughing. While he was a bit embarrassed himself at being caught kissing by his mother and Joanna, Carolyn was obviously traumatized by it. Just the small act of holding hands seemed enough to make her feel like a criminal.

Kyle let go of her hand. Carolyn smiled at him gratefully.

"It really is okay, though," he told her again.

"I know," she said apologetically. "I'm just a little freaked out, that's all."

Kyle smiled his understanding, hoping that Carolyn wouldn't stay so freaked out that she would try to get rid of him for good.

"Dennis's little girl is too cute," Carolyn said, changing the subject.

"Yeah," Kyle agreed. "But nowhere near as cute as you."

Carolyn started to blush as the compliment practically stopped her dead in her tracks.

She seemed so taken aback that Kyle wanted to kick himself again for saying something that probably just came off as sounding really goofy. But before he could figure out a way to take his foot out of his mouth, Carolyn's smile stole yet another little piece of his heart.

"You know what?" she said as she wrapped her hand back around his. "You're right. It is okay."

And as Carolyn squeezed his hand affectionately, Kyle Stoddard started to fly even higher than the airplane swing in the back of the yard.

CHAPTER 21

"Higher!" Alyssa squealed as a crowd of people gathered around to watch her.

"Look at me, Mommy!" The "precious little thing" cried for the attention of the one person whose admiration and devotion matters most to a child. "Look at me!"

Yeah, Mommy! The voice in Baby D's head echoed the same desperate need as she stood, a nameless, faceless, helpless little three-year-old lost among the crowd. *Look at me!*

Only Baby D's mommy wasn't looking at her at all. Baby D's mommy was looking at Dennis's little girl as she pushed her higher and higher, in Baby D's swing.

It was the swing that Baby D's daddy built. The swing that her mommy had promised would always be just for Baby D. But Baby D's mommy had told a lie. Yeah. Baby D's mommy had given Baby D's swing to her new baby, as if Baby D had never existed.

"More!" the "precious little thing" demanded as Baby D's mommy happily complied, oblivious to the devastation she was causing her own child.

It's my airplane, Mommy! The jealous screams echoed through Baby D's head as she stood tortured by the sight. *It's my airplane!*

Baby D would have given anything to push Dennis's little girl even higher than her mommy was pushing her. Yeah. Baby D wanted to push Dennis's little girl so high that she would fly right out of Baby D's airplane and go soaring across the yard until she landed head-first on the concrete walkway, cracking her precious little skull into a thousand tiny pieces. Pieces that no one would be able to fit back together again.

Baby D pulled her gaze away from her mommy in an effort to regain some control. But as her eyes darted about her own backyard, the sight of her mommy's new "baby" captured her attention. And within seconds, Baby D was starting to focus again. Because when it came right down to it, it wasn't really Dennis's little girl she wanted to kill at all.

CHAPTER 22

When Snake slithered up to the grill to get himself a second burger, he came alone. That made Mallory very nervous. Even in Dee Ann's presence, Snake's behavior with Mallory had been questionable at best. He'd stood so close to her and managed to brush up against her so many times, Mallory had felt more like she was packed onto a rush-hour subway car than standing in the middle of two acres of open space. As he came near her again, she began to feel claustrophobic.

"Well, hello again, darlin'." Snake looked her up and down, making her skin crawl.

"Mallory," she corrected him.

"You don't think for a minute that I could forget *your* name, do you, sugar?" Snake laughed.

Mallory just let it go. Even though she hated it when guys came on to her with that "sweetheart, honey, baby, sugar" stuff, she knew when to confront it and when to back off.

"Would you like another burger?" Mallory offered, taking a step back as Snake took one toward her.

"I want somethin'," he leered. "I'm just not sure exactly what yet. You ever get that way?"

"No," Mallory answered as matter-of-factly as she could, as if his question had been innocent. But nothing about Snake was innocent. And Mallory knew she had to be very careful not to give him any encouragement. "I always know exactly what I want."

"You're too young to be that way." He kept up his game of cat and mouse. "You got to learn to feel your way around a little bit. Try something new every now and then." He winked at her. "Ever been on a motorcycle?"

"No," she answered. Her eyes scanned the lawn, looking for Dee Ann. Finally she spotted her talking to another waitress. Only Dee Ann wasn't really talking. She was glaring at Mallory.

"Wanna go for a spin?" Snake asked Mallory.

"I don't think I'm up for that kind of danger," Mallory answered.

Snake laughed. "Bein' on a bike's not dangerous, darlin'. Not when I'm in control."

Now it was Mallory's turn to laugh. "Oh, I'm not afraid of the bike," she told him. "But Dee Ann's got me a little worried." She nodded her head in Dee Ann's direction.

Snake took a look. But instead of being chastened, he seemed amused, flattered even. "No, I guess you don't want to tangle with Dee Ann," he mused, as if Mallory were really considering fighting her for Snake's attention. "Trust me, in a fair fight, you'd lose. And Dee Ann don't fight fair," he added. "I guess you better give me a couple of burgers, so I can go over there and cool her jets before she turns ugly."

Mallory obliged, happy to get rid of Snake.

"Catch you later." He winked before heading off to placate Dee Ann.

"Carolyn!" Mallory called out when she noticed Carolyn standing by herself. It was the first time all day that Mallory had seen her without Kyle, and Mallory wanted to take the opportunity to find out how things were going between them. From what she'd observed, things were going pretty well. But the look on Carolyn's face as she approached Mallory told a very different story.

"What's wrong?" Mallory asked, alarmed.

"Nothing." Carolyn tried to smile.

"Something's wrong," Mallory insisted. "Is it Kyle?"

"No," Carolyn said emphatically.

"Then what?" Mallory pressed.

"You're not going to believe what just happened to me."

Mallory waited as Carolyn struggled to find the right words.

"Kyle and I were over by the swings . . . and he kissed me," she blurted out.

"So what's so bad about that?" Mallory asked. "That sounds like good news to me!"

"C. J. and your mother caught us," Carolyn delivered the bad news.

Mallory had to put her hand to her mouth to keep from laughing.

"It's not funny," Carolyn scolded.

"I know," Mallory apologized. "It's humiliating to get caught," she sympathized. "But it happens to everybody sooner or later. It's not really such a big deal."

"You didn't see the look on C. J.'s face," Carolyn groaned.

Out of the corner of her eye, Mallory saw her mother approaching them. But Carolyn didn't notice Joanna and went on talking.

"It was a nightmare," Carolyn told Mallory. "Humiliating doesn't even begin to describe it. I can't even imagine what C. J. must think. I'm sure she hates me."

"C. J.?" Joanna sounded surprised as she stepped up beside Carolyn. "What on earth would make you think that C. J. hates you?"

Carolyn blushed. Mallory wanted to spill her guts, knowing that her mother would make it better, but she kept quiet in deference to Carolyn.

Joanna was smart enough to know what was going on, and sensitive enough to handle it just right. "You mean because of what happened back there?" She nodded toward the swings.

Carolyn nodded guiltily.

"Oh, honey." Joanna laughed, putting her arm around Carolyn's shoulder. "That's nothing to be upset about. And it's certainly no reason to think that C. J. hates you."

Carolyn's face said that she wasn't convinced.

"I happen to know that C. J. likes you very much," Joanna went on. "She's said so many, many times."

Carolyn's expression began to brighten.

"The fact that you're dating her son isn't going to change her feelings about you," Joanna explained. "C. J.'s a bigger person than that. I know she seems tough on the outside. But believe me, you won't find a kinder, more gentle human being."

"That's for sure," Mallory agreed with her mother.

"I just don't want C. J. to think badly of me," Carolyn said.

"Nobody could think badly of you," Joanna assured her. "Now, you'd better cheer up, because I see Prince Charming headed this way," she teased Carolyn.

Kyle was indeed headed in their direction. And he was coming fast.

"Run!" Mallory shrieked, recognizing the look

on Kyle's face. She pushed Carolyn to get her moving. "He's gonna throw somebody in the pool!"

Mallory heard Carolyn laugh as the two of them took off in different directions. Mallory laughed, too, thinking that the peaceful afternoon was over.

The picnic was about to turn into Helter-Skelter.

CHAPTER 23

Renee had never seen so many people having so much fun. Yeah, this was the life. It was the life that Mallory had enjoyed from the moment she was born. It was the life that Renee should have had, could have had, would have had, but for a simple accident of birth.

That was all it came down to really. An accident of birth. It was what separated princes from paupers, as surely as it separated Mallory from Renee.

An accident. Certainly not Mallory's fault. She'd no more chosen the paths of their lives than Renee had. Still, Renee just couldn't seem to forgive her.

Renee didn't like being so bitter. In fact, it was the one thing she hated most about herself. But it wasn't Renee's fault that her soul was even more scarred than her body. Hard lives made hard people. And Renee's life had been hard. Real hard.

She'd hoped that she could just walk away from her old life, leave it behind like a hermit crab leaves its shell when it finds a better one. She'd hoped that she could move into her new life fresh and clean. But it didn't work that way.

Renee didn't fit into her new life. The life she'd always dreamed of turned out to be full of heartache, disappointment, and loneliness. Maybe it was her. Maybe the capacity for happiness had been beaten out of her long ago. Maybe she simply did not possess the skills it took to survive in the kind of world where "nice" people lived.

These were nice people. No doubt about that. Even Mallory, Renee had to admit, was nice. Really nice. Genuinely nice. Not "nice" the way Renee was "nice." "Nice" for Renee was only a facade behind which she hid the fact that most of the time she was seething. In Renee's case, it wasn't the shell that was defective, it was what lived inside.

Renee's only hope was that if she pretended long enough and hard enough, she would eventually become what she pretended to be. But for now, pretending was all she had.

It wasn't easy always pretending, always being on guard. But Renee couldn't afford a slipup. She didn't want anybody to know who she really was, or where she *really* came from. So far, Renee thought, she had managed to put on a pretty good show.

Only Mallory seemed suspicious. Renee knew that Mallory could sense her animosity. That was a problem. If Renee couldn't make herself feel less resentful of Mallory, she would simply have to hide it better. Renee was determined to buddy-up to Mallory if it killed her.

That was why Renee pretended to try to free Mallory from Kyle's grip as he carried her to the edge of the pool to drop her in. Once he'd tossed Mallory in, Kyle made a grab for Renee. But she eluded him nicely, and he found another victim. Within seconds, people were going into the pool left and right.

Over the sound of screams and laughter, Renee heard Mallory calling to her.

"Renee!" Mallory had made her way to the edge of the pool. She was reaching her hand out of the water. "Renee! Help me out!"

Renee hesitated for just an instant. But then she steeled herself and reached out for Mallory.

CHAPTER 24

Mallory smiled as she grabbed hold of Renee's hand with no intention of trying to climb out of the pool. It was payback time. And Renee was about to pay big.

"Just remember," Renee joked as she tightened her grip around Mallory's hand and positioned her footing so that she could yank Mallory out of the pool. "You owe me one for this."

Mallory almost cracked up. Renee seemed totally oblivious to the fact that that was exactly what Mallory was remembering . . . owing her one.

"Hey." Renee laughed as she gave Mallory a tug. "You've gotta help me out a little bit," she told her, rebracing her footing to try again.

Only Mallory wasn't budging. Because Mallory had done some foot bracing of her own—against the wall of the pool. That way she could get the leverage she needed to tug back even harder. And much more successfully.

"Man," Renee huffed, refusing to give up. "If you weren't so skinny, I'd be suggesting some kind of diet plan. How about I count to three," she said, catching her breath. "And on three," she told Mallory, "you try to jump out."

"Okay," Mallory agreed.

"One . . ." Renee started to count, "two . . ."

Mallory was ready for the big moment.

"Three!" Renee started to pull. "Jump out!"

"I don't think so!" Mallory teased. And as she yanked Renee forward, she watched the expression on Renee's face turn from innocent and unsuspecting to shocked, stunned, and amazed. "I caught you!" Mallory declared victoriously.

Before Renee even had a chance to object, Mallory yanked her straight over her shoulder and into the deep end of the pool.

Renee didn't bend into what should have been a dive. Instead, she tried to stop the inevitable, hitting the water hard, in one of silliest-looking belly flops Mallory had ever seen. It left Mallory in hysterics, feeling more than a little pleased with herself and her newly found feelings of friendship for Renee.

But Renee wasn't laughing. At least not yet anyway. In fact, Mallory could see that Renee still looked shocked. She was flailing about the center of the pool as if she were trying to get her bearings.

"Hey, Renee," Mallory called out as she started to swim toward her. "I guess we're even now, huh?"

The look Renee shot Mallory was anything but amused. Before Mallory even had a chance to reach her, Renee disappeared under the water.

Mallory had the horrible feeling that maybe she'd pushed Renee's happy picnic persona a little too far. Then she felt the hands wrap around her ankle.

Mallory barely had a chance to catch her breath before Renee yanked her under. She was a little startled by Renee's desire to get even, but mostly she was relieved. Apparently Renee wasn't as angry as Mallory had first thought. If Renee wanted to have the last laugh, Mallory would let her. When they both came back up again, Mallory would let Renee crack up in her face.

But Renee wasn't coming back up. And neither was Mallory—Renee wasn't letting go of her ankle.

Mallory was starting to run out of air as Renee seemed to be struggling to pull her to the bottom of the pool. If Renee was trying to be funny, Mallory wasn't at all amused. Not anymore. In fact, Renee's actions were starting to feel uncomfortably mean and downright malicious.

Mallory jerked her leg frantically, trying to send the message that this wasn't a joke, that she had to let go. But Renee refused to let go. Mallory started to panic. The pressure in her lungs was getting to be too much to bear.

She reached down and grabbed the collar of the shirt Renee was wearing over her bathing suit, yanking it upward with all of her might. As Renee finally released the grip she had around Mallory's ankle, Mallory started to kick furiously in an effort to resurface. Her body's need for oxygen sent urgent signals to her brain to immediately fill her lungs. But Mallory was determined not to let that happen until her head was out of the water.

Mallory looked toward the surface of the pool, her lungs burning. While the six or seven feet she had to go seemed more like six or seven miles, Mallory assured herself that she would make it.

Then she felt Renee grab the waistband of her shorts, yanking her two feet back down again. In that one instant, there was no doubt left in Mallory's mind that Renee was trying to drown her.

Mallory reached down and grabbed a fistful of Renee's hair, pulling so hard that she was sure she was hurting Renee. But Mallory didn't care, because Renee didn't seem to care that she was hurting Mallory.

With the kind of adrenaline that only starts pumping out of fear of death, Mallory managed to pull herself and Renee, despite Renee's clinging and clawing, all the way up to the surface of the pool.

But before Mallory's entire face was out of water, her breathing reflexes took over. She gulped in as much water as air, causing more pain than relief.

Renee was gasping for air as well as she wrapped her arm around Mallory's throat.

"Get off me!" Mallory lashed out as she pushed Renee away.

Renee fought back, struggling to regain her hold on Mallory.

But Mallory wasn't about to let that happen. This time Mallory kicked Renee hard, using Renee's body as a springboard to propel herself toward the side of the pool.

"What the heck is going on with you two?"

Mallory saw Carolyn standing on the side of the pool, looking concerned.

"Are you all right?"

"No!" Mallory gasped. It took all of her strength to lift herself out of the water. "That girl is out of her mind." She choked out the words. "I swear, she was trying to kill me or something." Mallory glanced back toward Renee. But Renee was nowhere to be seen.

"Oh, my God, Mallory," Carolyn gasped. "I thought you guys were just fooling around." Carolyn kicked off her sneakers frantically. "I think she's drowning, Mal!"

Mallory's heart suddenly felt as constricted as her breathing. Carolyn dove straight over her head toward the shadowy figure of Renee, who was sinking to the bottom of the pool.

CHAPTER 25

"Out of my way, girlie," Trudy ordered as she elbowed her way past Dee Ann toward the crowd that was starting to gather around Carolyn and Renee. "I'm CPR certified."

If Dee Ann hadn't been so irritated, she probably would have laughed in Trudy's face. "She's standing up, for Pete's sakes, Trudy," Dee Ann snapped. "She doesn't need to be rescued anymore."

But Dee Ann's remarks landed on Trudy's back with less of an impact than a mosquito slamming into an elephant's behind. Trudy rushed over to Renee's side, along with everybody else.

Just the sight of Joanna coddling Renee was enough to make Dee Ann want to puke. Renee didn't deserve to be coddled. She deserved to be dead. As far as Dee Ann was concerned, Renee Dixon should have drowned—just for being so stupid.

But Dee Ann wasn't totally convinced that that was the case as she watched Renee refuse the comfort of everyone around her but Joanna. No.

Renee Dixon wasn't stupid at all. In fact, Dee Ann was starting to feel awfully sorry that she hadn't planned a little drowning episode of her own; Renee was getting the kind of attention Dee Ann would have killed for.

And Renee wasn't the only one.

Dee Ann managed to tear her eyes away from Renee as Joanna started to lead her toward the house. Someone else caught her attention.

The sight of Mallory standing by the side of the pool, "Snake"-charming, was enough to send Dee Ann into a murderous rage.

"I'm tellin' you, darlin'." Snake's eyes were so focused on Mallory's anatomy that he didn't notice Dee Ann storming up behind him. "You got nothin' to feel bad about."

Mallory wasn't at all focused on Snake. In fact, her back was turned to him. But Snake didn't seem to care. And neither did Dee Ann.

"But if you want yourself a shoulder to cry on," Snake continued to leer, "I got two good ones right here. And I guarantee you, sugar," he slithered a little closer to Mallory, reaching up to put his hands on her shoulders, "a couple of minutes in my arms, and you'll start to feel a whole lot better than good."

Mallory pulled away immediately, spinning around to face yet another assault as Dee Ann started to bare her own fangs.

"Gee, Mallory." Dee Ann went straight for the jugular. "Don't you have enough toys back here to play with?"

Mallory didn't respond; she just stared at Dee Ann, dumbfounded.

"Don't start, Dee Ann." Snake wrapped his leathery fingers tightly around her wrist.

"No," Dee Ann snapped back. "Don't *you* start!"

"You've gotta forgive Dee Ann." Snake smiled at Mallory before he glared back at Dee Ann. "See, Dee Ann here just feels awfully inadequate around you, don't you, Dee Ann?"

Snake's fangs were a whole lot bigger and a whole lot sharper than Dee Ann's. And the poisonous look in Snake's eyes told Dee Ann that it was definitely time for her to retract her own fangs.

"Especially in that wet bathin' suit of yours," he told Mallory. "You gotta admit, darlin'," he smiled maliciously at Dee Ann, "there ain't no way, even with the kind of money these people have, that you could buy yourself a body like that."

The embarrassed look Mallory shot Dee Ann as she turned and walked away was enough to make Dee Ann loathe Mallory all the more. She knew that Mallory was cringing at Snake's advances. And she also knew that Mallory wasn't embarrassed for herself—she was embarrassed for Dee Ann.

"Don't flatter yourself, Mallory," Dee Ann called after her. "If you think for one minute he was serious, think again. He was goofin' on *you*, you idiot." Dee Ann could feel the angry tears starting to rise. "Not me!"

Snake laughed condescendingly. "You tell her, darlin'."

Dee Ann tried to pull away from Snake's viselike grip, but Snake refused to let go, practically crushing her wrist.

As Dee Ann really did burst into tears, she wanted to murder Snake with all of her heart.

Snake didn't care about Dee Ann. Not anymore. The only thing Snake seemed to care about protecting these days was the free ride Dee Ann was willing to provide. Problem was, Dee Ann was getting awfully tired of paying the price.

Thanks to Mallory, Dee Ann was finally ready to find a way to get Snake out of her life for good. And while Snake had let Dee Ann know that he would kill her before he ever let her walk away, Dee Ann was more than willing to do whatever it took to protect her own life now. Even if it meant taking Snake's.

CHAPTER 26

Renee couldn't stop shaking. It was as if her bones were made of ice, as if they were freezing her from the inside out. The terror would not subside.

"It's all right," Joanna comforted her, wrapping a big blanket around Renee. "You're okay now."

But Renee's mind couldn't comprehend that. She just sat on her bed staring off into space, thinking how close she had come to death—at Mallory's hand.

Even in a state of shock, Renee could appreciate the irony of that. She wanted to laugh at the absurdity of it all; she had survived so much only to almost be done in by a practical joke.

But Renee didn't laugh. Instead, she burst into tears.

"It's okay," Joanna said, sitting down on the bed. She took Renee in her arms and began to rock gently back and forth. "You go ahead and cry," she told Renee.

But Renee didn't want to cry. She'd lost enough dignity for one day. What a spectacle she mus have been. The poor, underprivileged kid who couldn't even swim, flailing around, fighting for her life. Not really so different from her day-to-day existence, she thought bitterly.

"You must have been so frightened." Joanna's voice was soothing, and she was stroking Renee's hair. "But you're safe now." Joanna held her even tighter, as if to prove it.

It had been a long, long time since Renee had been held like that. A long, long time since she'd known such warmth, and comfort, and safety.

The last little bit of Renee's dignity crumbled, and she melted against Joanna, sobbing uncontrollably. In a strange way, it felt good. Pent-up emotion poured out with the tears that streamed down her face.

Renee cried until she was exhausted. And even then Joanna continued to hold her. Joanna didn't have much choice really. Renee was clinging to her desperately.

Renee knew that she ought to let go. But she couldn't. For one brief moment, Renee had the thing she longed for, the thing she needed most. A mother. A real mother.

CHAPTER 27

Joanna's heart ached for the child who was sobbing in her arms . . . and for the child she'd left outside.

Poor Mallory, she thought as she comforted Renee. Joanna wanted to be able to comfort her daughter too. She knew that Mallory was suffering every bit as much as Renee was. Maybe even more.

Mallory did not forgive herself easily. Joanna knew that Mallory would berate herself endlessly for the stupidity of what she'd done. But it wasn't stupid. Not really. How could Mallory have known that Renee couldn't swim? Perhaps it was a mistake to have assumed that she could. But it was a reasonable assumption, an assumption that Joanna herself made, an assumption that Renee's behavior inspired. No, Mallory wasn't to blame for what had happened. But convincing Mallory of that was going to be a task. And unfortunately, it was going to have to wait.

As much as Joanna wanted to go to her daughter, she couldn't dream of leaving Renee.

Renee's needs were greater. Greater than Joanna had imagined.

Renee was so desperate to prove that she fit in, she was willing to risk her life to do it. She'd been up by that pool, dressed in a bathing suit, acting as if she belonged there. And she'd never admitted to anyone that she didn't know how to swim. Joanna couldn't stop wondering what would possess Renee to keep such a thing secret.

But Renee had lots of secrets. Joanna was sure of it. Dark, dangerous secrets. The kinds of secrets that eat away at a person the way termites destroy a house, silent and unseen—at least until now.

Joanna had seen something out by the pool that disturbed her very much. It was something she wasn't meant to see, something that Renee took great pains to hide. And If it hadn't been for the accident, Renee's ugly secret would have been safe. But when Renee's bathing suit cover-up came off during her struggle in the pool, it revealed a body covered with scars. Not the kinds of scars left by childhood play. No, these scars were evidence of violence. There were cuts and burns. More than anything, Joanna wanted to ask Renee how those scars had gotten there. What kind of monster would inflict such injury?

But Joanna swallowed the question over and over again. Not because she wanted to close her eyes to it. Not because she felt it wasn't her responsibility, or her business. But because she was afraid Renee was too fragile to face it. Now was not the time to pick at old wounds and make them bleed again. Joanna could not bear to hurt Renee any more than she had been hurt already.

"You're safe now," Joanna whispered. She wrapped her arms even more tightly around Renee, as if to prove that it was true.

It was true. Joanna would protect Renee as if she were her own child. As long as Renee was in Joanna's custody, living under Joanna's roof, she was safe. Joanna promised herself that somehow she would see to it that nobody would ever hurt Renee again.

CHAPTER 28

"Guess what day it is, Your Honor?" Baby D couldn't help laughing as she dragged the body of Judge Kramer's twelve-year-old son toward the deserted shack that housed the remains of Dr. Elaine Baxter's little girl. Two feet under the same corroded old floorboard lay Jack Riley's "baby."

"It's judgment day." Baby D answered her own question. "But, guess what?" Baby D struggled to pull the limp body through a thicket of dead branches. "This time it's *my* honor." Baby D cracked herself up as she finally managed to maneuver the body onto easier ground. "This time, *I'm* sittin' on the bench. And guess whose innocent little life is in my hands?"

This was going to be a judgment day the less-than-honorable Helen R. Kramer would remember for the rest of her life. In fact, Baby D was quite certain that by tomorrow morning, Judge Kramer was going to be wishing with all of her heart that September twenty-first had never existed.

Baby D kicked open the door to the shack as she started to play out her own little courtroom drama.

"After years of painful deliberation, it is the decision of this court that this child be removed from the custody of Judge Helen R. Kramer for all eternity . . ."

Baby D maneuvered Judge Kramer's son over toward the rotting floorboard that would conceal his grave.

"And while it would truly please this court no end to be able to place this child in the custody of Lorene and Calvin Burnell, so that little Baby K here might understand firsthand the sins of his mommy's decision, the court has no choice but to remand custody to a higher power."

Baby D pulled up the floorboard as she gave voice to the same objections the defense attorneys had made in her behalf.

"But, Your Honor," Baby D mocked, "in the interest of the child, I would implore the court to grant a motion for reconsideration . . ."

Baby D laughed as she cut a clump of hair from Judge Kramer's son's head.

"Sorry. Motion denied."

Yeah. Baby D was planning to be just as kind in handing down her own decision as Judge Kramer had been in handing down Baby D's.

"I'd like then to request a motion for a stay, pending appeal . . ."

Baby D cracked herself up again as she shoved the clump of hair into her pocket and rolled the body into the grave.

"Sorry, again."

Baby D stood up, smiling down at the body. "That motion is also denied."

Thanks to Judge Kramer, every motion was denied. There was no "reconsideration." In fact, there seemed to be no consideration at all. The defense attorneys had practically begged Judge Kramer for a "stay," so Baby D's adoptive parents could prepare themselves and Baby D for the traumatic separation, but Judge Kramer remained unmoved. Her final decision stood, leaving Baby D's adoptive parents with little more than a week's time to say good-bye to the little girl they'd nurtured and adored.

"And guess who else isn't getting a stay or an appeal?" Baby D remained as unmoved as Judge Kramer as she pulled the gun from the waist of her jeans.

Baby D laughed as she fired the first round, taking careful aim to make sure that she'd stolen the last bit of life Judge Kramer's kid was hanging on to. When she was sure her own decision would stand, Baby D replaced the old floorboard and headed back into the woods.

For the first time in her life, September twenty-first felt more like a cause for celebration than a day of mourning. In little more than a week's time, Baby D would add the weight of one last "baby" to the scales of justice, balancing them for good.

CHAPTER 29

Mallory sat alone in the dark. She listened to the old swing creak as she rocked herself, trying to find some comfort. But there was none. Her life was falling to pieces and there was nothing she could do about it.

Mallory was a displaced person. She didn't seem to belong anywhere anymore, not even in her own home. Ever since the accident, her mother did nothing but dote on Renee. Half the time she didn't even seem to notice that Mallory still lived there too.

It wasn't that her mother blamed Mallory for the accident. In fact, she'd gone to great pains to convince Mallory to put it behind her. Even Renee had forgiven Mallory. She'd said that there was nothing to forgive. Renee had insisted that she was more responsible for what had happened than Mallory was. That was what she'd said, and she'd certainly sounded sincere about it. Still, Renee continued to keep her distance. By now Mallory had given up any hope of a true friendship between them.

Then there was Kyle. He and Carolyn had

begun spending a lot of time together. All their free time, in fact.

From where she was sitting, Mallory could see the two of them inside Kyle's house. They were in the den together, watching TV. Mallory could have gone over there. She would have been more than welcome. Both Kyle and Carolyn went out of their way to include her. But she knew that even if she went over there, she would still end up feeling every bit as lonely as if she just stayed where she was.

Mallory tried not to pay attention to Kyle and Carolyn. She felt creepy watching them, like a peeping Tom. But she couldn't seem to stop herself. They were sitting there on the big, over-stuffed couch, talking and laughing, the way Kyle and Mallory always had

Carolyn certainly seemed very much at home in Kyle's house. And Mallory realized with some surprise that she felt jealous. Carolyn was where Mallory ought to have been. Carolyn had taken her place.

Mallory tried to tell herself that it was silly to feel that way. After all, it was she who had pushed Kyle and Carolyn together in the first place. And it wasn't as if she had ever considered a romantic relationship with Kyle. She had just never considered life without Kyle. She took it for granted that she would always come first with him, the way he came first with her. But things were changing, and they were changing way too fast.

As Mallory sat feeling sorry for herself, the Stoddards' kitchen door opened and C. J. stepped out onto the deck. Mallory watched as C. J. walked to the edge of the deck, leaned against the railing, and looked up at the stars. Standing there like that, C. J. seemed every bit as lonely as Mallory.

Mallory thought about going over to talk to C. J., but then she thought that maybe C. J. wanted to be alone. So she stayed where she was, hidden in the shadows.

But when C. J. stepped off the deck and started across the grass, Mallory changed her mind. She was about to call out to C. J., when C. J. stopped in the middle of the lawn and lit a cigarette.

Now they were both in an embarrassing situation. C. J. had quit smoking over a year ago, but recently Mallory had thought she occasionally smelled smoke on C. J.

C. J. was headed in Mallory's direction, and Mallory had no choice but to make her presence known. "C. J.," Mallory called out timidly.

C. J. dropped her cigarette and stepped on it. "Mallory? Is that you?" she called out as she kept walking toward the swing set.

"Yeah," Mallory answered. "It's me."

"I guess you caught me," C. J. said guiltily.

"Afraid so." Mallory felt just as guilty, though she wasn't quite sure why. Sometimes it was just as bad to catch somebody as it was to get caught.

"You're not going to rat on me, are you?" C. J. asked.

"I ought to," Mallory answered playfully. "But I won't."

"You're a good kid." C. J. laughed, sitting down on the swing next to Mallory's.

Mallory couldn't help noticing the way C. J. touched the airplane swing as she passed it. From time to time, she'd seen her mother do the very same thing.

"So, what are you doing out here all by yourself?" C. J. went on.

Mallory didn't have an answer, and she couldn't lie to C. J., so she just shrugged.

"You're having a tough time, aren't you, Mal?" C. J. was never one to beat around the bush.

There was no use denying it. Mallory nodded.

"I know." C. J. patted Mallory's leg affectionately. "So does your mom."

"I don't think she does," Mallory said, hoping that she didn't sound like a spoiled brat.

"Sure she does," C. J. assured her. "Your mom's a smart woman. And a sensitive one. She knows that this situation with Renee is hard on you. It isn't easy on her either. She's really got her hands full with that kid."

"Why does she always do this?" Mallory sighed.

"Do what?" C. J. asked.

"Volunteer to have other kids come live with us," Mallory answered. "It's like I'm not enough for her."

"Oh, Mal, that's not it at all," C. J. assured her. "Your mom loves you more than anything else in this whole world. You know that. But your mom always dreamed of having a big family. She wanted lots of kids. She just couldn't have them."

"Did she ever think about adopting?" Mallory asked.

"Before you were born," C. J. answered. "But there were all kinds of problems."

Mallory got the sense that there was a long story, and she waited for C. J. to tell it. C. J. was quiet for a moment, frowning thoughtfully, or maybe sadly; Mallory couldn't be sure which it was. But then C. J. just seemed to shake off the thought.

"Anyway." C. J. smiled again. "You came along. And you were enough. More than enough. And don't you ever doubt that. You're everything your mother ever dreamed of in a daughter, Mal. Everything I ever dreamed of too."

"You're a good mom, C. J." Mallory smiled, feeling a whole lot better, and certainly less alone.

"Do me a favor," C. J. said. "Go inside and tell

that to somebody else. She needs to hear it, because she's feeling as insecure as you are these days. Your mother needs you every bit as much as you need her, Mal. Don't let anything, or anybody, come between you."

CHAPTER 30

Renee was on her way upstairs when she heard voices coming from Joanna's room. Instinctively, she stopped and listened. The voices were muffled. But Renee knew that it was Joanna and Mallory talking. It had to be. There was no one else in the house except Ryan Dunne, and he was downstairs in his study, occupied with paperwork.

Renee began to move up the steps slowly and silently. As she neared the top of the stairs, she began to hear the conversation more clearly. The first intelligible sentence stopped Renee dead in her tracks.

"I know you're feeling neglected, Mal," Joanna said.

Neglected! Renee wanted to laugh. Mallory hadn't the first clue what "neglected" felt like. Still, Renee predicted with dead-on accuracy what Mallory's answer would be.

"A little." Mallory's voice made it sound like more than just a little.

"I'm sorry," Joanna said. "I really am. I had no idea this would be so difficult. I think we just need to give Renee a little more time to adjust."

"I don't think she's ever going to adjust to me," Mallory said hopelessly.

She's got that right, Renee thought with a smirk.

"Go easy on her, Mal."

There was a hint of reprimand in Joanna's voice, and it made Renee feel good that Joanna was taking her side.

But Mallory didn't seem to feel very good about that. "I've tried," she protested. "I've done everything I can to be nice to her, to make her like me. I feel like I spend all day, every day, tiptoeing around that girl, trying to make sure I don't do anything to hurt her feelings. I just wish somebody was worried about *my* feelings."

Renee was waiting for Joanna to blow up, to tell Mallory what a spoiled brat she sounded like. But that didn't happen.

"Oh, sweetheart," Joanna cooed instead. "*I'm* worried about your feelings. I know it may not seem that way to you lately. I know I've been giving a lot more time and energy to Renee. But, Mallory, *you* are my daughter. And no one is more important to me than you are. I'm sorry if I've been taking you for granted. I guess I don't tell you nearly enough how much I love you, and how very proud of you I am. But you've got to know that even when I seem faraway and distracted, you're always on my mind, and always, always in my heart."

It was quiet then. Renee could just picture Joanna holding Mallory the same way she'd held Renee after the accident. Funny how it took a life-threatening experience for Renee to get what came to Mallory so freely.

"I love you, Mommy," Mallory said.

Renee decided that she'd heard enough. More than enough. She stole up the last few steps and down the hallway into her room, where she closed the door soundlessly and locked it.

Renee had never felt more alone than she did at that moment, or more aware of all she'd lost. The only comfort to be found was in a box that she kept carefully hidden away. She got it now, and sat down on the bed, clutching it tightly.

Inside that box was her most prized possession, a talisman of sorts. It gave her strength and kept her going through unspeakable horrors. It was proof to her that once upon a time someone loved her the way a child ought to be loved, the way Joanna loved Mallory.

Renee hesitated before opening the box. She always did. She was always afraid of what she would feel—or not feel. What if the charm had lost its magic over her?

Renee took a deep breath and lifted the lid of the velvet jewelry box. Inside was a small, silver locket. It couldn't have weighed more than a few ounces. But for Renee, it was an anchor. Just looking at it reminded her of who she was and why she was there.

CHAPTER 31

"**I**t's ten o'clock, Judge Kramer." Trudy Zigler checked her watch again as she folded the newspaper she was scanning and hit the remote to turn on her TV. "Let's see if you still think you know where your children are," she said grimly.

There had been no reports about Judge Kramer all day. None. Not in the late edition of the local newspaper, not on the radio, not on TV. Trudy was sure of it. She had been tuning in to the local radio station all day at the deli, listening to the news at the top of every hour; and now that she was home, she was tuning in to the local cable station just as frequently. While September twenty-first seemed to be ticking away without incident, Trudy was willing to bet her life that there was no way in the world Judge Kramer was going to bed tonight with all her children accounted for. And it was more than just a hunch.

"In local news tonight, another child has been reported missing in Dearfield County . . ."

Trudy turned up the volume. She knew exactly whose child it was.

"Carl Kramer, Jr., the twelve-year-old son of Dr. Carl M. Kramer and the Honorable Helen R. Kramer, was reported missing shortly after eight P.M. this evening by Judge Kramer. The child was last seen at approximately six A.M. by the Kramers' live-in housekeeper shortly before the child left the house on his paper route with the intention of heading straight to school. Due to an oversight, authorities at Morgan Elementary School failed to notify the parents of the child's absence, thereby allowing more than twelve hours to elapse before Judge Kramer realized the child was missing . . ."

"That's it, Judge," Trudy said. "Blame it on the school system this time. I mean, heaven forbid you should blame yourself for a change."

Trudy had half a mind to pick up the phone and call the local cable station, to point out to their shoddy reporter just whose negligence really was responsible for little Jr.'s predicament. Trudy was dying to tell the whole world just how negligent Helen R. Kramer really was—in more ways than one.

Helen R. Kramer had been the youngest attorney in the history of the state to be appointed to a superior court judgeship. She was also the first woman in the county ever named to the bench. While those two accomplishments irritated many of her male peers, Helen R. Kramer's appointment to the court won the praise and admiration of almost every female in the state. Including Trudy.

When Helen R. Kramer was chosen to preside over the Baby D case not two months after her appointment, Trudy was thrilled. While Trudy hardly considered herself a feminist, she couldn't help thinking that having a woman on the bench, a woman who was a young mother herself at the time, would improve the odds of insuring justice. Trudy was sure that Judge Helen R. Kramer would find a way to use her head and rule with her heart, looking beyond biology and opting for the basics. Trudy was sure Judge Kramer would understand that "Mommy" was a title even more hard-won than "Your Honor."

But Trudy was wrong. Helen Kramer's heart was wrapped up in protecting the title that earned her the prestige. Even with all the facts in hand, including the arrest record of Calvin Burnell, a record Trudy had seen with her own eyes, Helen Kramer refused to jeopardize her standing in her male-dominated profession. She had been afraid she would put herself in a position where some cheap reporter could accuse her of being biased because of her gender. The law was the law. Judge Helen R. Kramer insisted the system itself was to blame, that she had no choice in her decision.

"While the disappearance of Carl Kramer, Jr. marks the second disappearance in Dearfield County in the last two months," the TV newscaster said, "police are treating each case separately, insisting that there is no evidence at this time to suggest connection between the two . . ."

"Three." Trudy corrected the report that failed to take into account Jack Riley's little girl. "There are three missing kids, you idiot. And if the connection were any clearer, it'd bite you on the behind."

"Anyone with information . . ."

"Yeah, yeah, yeah," Trudy mocked as she cut off the report, hitting the remote to turn off the TV. "Trust me," Trudy rambled to herself as she got up from the couch and headed into the kitchen. "You ain't gettin' any information, because you people don't know what to do with it anyway."

Trudy headed for the refrigerator door, where she'd hung her big cat calendar. Usually she didn't like to see the new "Cat of the Month" before it was time to turn to the next month, but today she didn't have a choice. She had to see what day of the week October first would fall on. The first was little more than a week away, and Trudy was going to need the day off—to make the next, and final, connection.

CHAPTER

32

Baby D opened her eyes to what was definitely going to be the first day of the rest of her life. *Her* life. The life she would have been living all along. The life that Elaine Baxter and Jack Riley and Helen Kramer cared so little about.

The monsters of the past were still looming over her head, the way they had every past October first morning. But today Baby D found comfort in the fact that this time around, the monsters themselves would be tortured. This time around, the monsters would spend the day—and every other day for the rest of their lives—almost as tortured as Baby D.

Yeah. Baby D was getting a real big kick out of the fact that Babies B, R, and K were not going home today. The only baby going home today was Baby D. And wouldn't the monsters be surprised.

Baby D got out of the bed she was planning to strip for good and headed toward the window. She smiled as she watched the most beautiful sunrise she'd ever seen—more beautiful even than the one that had risen over the remains of Calvin and

Lorene Burnell. Today was going to be the most triumphant day of her life—and the happiest day of her mommy's. Before the day was through, the past would be totally erased, and Baby D's entire future would be rewritten—the right way.

As she stood there anticipating the wonderful events of the day, Baby D actually started to let some of the monsters go. She even found herself having some fond feelings for the biggest and baddest of them all—Calvin Burnell.

Thanks to Calvin Burnell, making sure that Mommy's better baby would be dead long before the sun set would be a piece of cake for Baby D. In fact, Baby D had to laugh at the idea that a piece of cake was probably a pretty good way to get Mommy's better baby to swallow the "medicine" Calvin Burnell had unwittingly willed to Baby D. But while lacing a slice of cake with Calvin Burnell's "wonder drug" was appealing to Baby D, she knew that it would be much more difficult to finesse than just dropping it into a cup of milk. Besides, Baby D had no time to be baking cakes today. No. Baby D would probably have to give the baby the medicine the same way Calvin Burnell used to give it to her.

It wasn't really medicine. At least not medicine that had been prescribed for the Burnells. The medicine Calvin Burnell gave Baby D was a drug prescribed for one of his biker buddy's "little seizure problems," mixed with some "expensive medicine" Calvin Burnell bought off the street. At first he used to give Baby D the seizure medicine alone to keep her quiet. But the seizure medicine just left Baby D lethargic, not incapacitated. And incapacitated was what Calvin and Lorene Burnell were shooting for. Yeah. It wasn't until Calvin Burnell accidentally gave Baby D the "expensive medicine" that he discovered his "wonder drug." He used to scream at Baby D for his having to waste "good money" on her wonder drug, until Lorene Burnell pointed out that they were actually saving money, because thanks to the "wonder drug," they'd never had to hire baby-sitters. Once they got that medicine down Baby D's throat, Baby D was totally incapacitated in less than forty-five minutes. Once Baby D's body stopped convulsing, which usually only lasted a minute or two, every muscle would go rigid, leaving Baby D paralyzed from the neck down for at least a couple of hours.

And a couple of hours was more than enough time for Baby D to kill the better baby and steal back her own life. Thanks to Calvin Burnell, there wasn't even going to be a struggle. No. Mommy's better baby wouldn't even have a chance to fight for the life that belonged to Baby D.

Baby D opened the dresser and pulled out the box where she'd kept all the pieces—the pieces of the life she was putting back together as well as the pieces of the lives she had shattered. As she started to pull the plastic bags containing the hair of Babies B, R, and K out of the box so she could wrap them up pretty for her mommy, Baby D smiled, anticipating her mommy's surprised reaction. Baby D was certain that her mommy was going to be so proud of her—and so happy.

But Baby D wasn't going to tell her mommy about what she had done to the other baby. Not today anyway. No. Baby D was just going to let her mommy think that the other baby had run away or something. It would be better for her mommy that way. And while Baby D was still pretty mad at her mommy for acting like she really loved the other baby, she was sure that her mommy was just pretending. She was probably just making believe that the other baby was Baby D. Once Baby D was back in her mommy's arms for good, her mommy would forget all about the other baby. And maybe then Baby D would tell her the truth. Maybe then Baby D would even give her mommy the last little bag she was planning to fill.

Baby D pulled the shiny pink ribbon from the box—the ribbon her mommy would tie in her hair for her—the way she always used to. Yeah. Only her mommy could tie the bow the right way so that Baby D would look pretty.

And Baby D wanted to look pretty.

Baby D turned her attention away from the box

and headed for the closet, terrified that she wouldn't have anything to wear that would make her look pretty enough. As she searched the closet for something special, something her mommy would like, something that would make her look just as pretty as Mallory Dunne . . . no . . . even prettier, so that her mommy would realize just how lucky she really was, Baby D started to panic. She became more and more frustrated as she pulled one garment after another from the wire hangers that lined the closet, irritated by the sight of everything she owned.

Baby D didn't have anything pretty. No. Baby D didn't have anything that looked half as pretty as the clothes Mallory had. The clothes that were way too nice to put on wire hangers.

Baby D began tearing the clothes from the closet so violently that the wire around the neck of the hangers ripped straight through the material. When most of the hangers were bare, Baby D collapsed to the floor in tears.

There were so many emotions surfacing simultaneously, Baby D was starting to lose it. By the time she finally remembered the dress that she'd bought for just this occasion—the very first day she blew into town—she'd already ripped all of the clothes on the floor in front of her to shreds.

But that was okay. Baby D wasn't going to need the rest of those stupid clothes anymore anyway. Baby D's mommy would buy her new clothes—clothes that would be even better than Mallory's. And Baby D would make her mommy buy her special hangers for them too.

As Baby D started to pull herself back together, assuring herself that everything was going to go according to plan, she headed back over to the box and pulled out the silver locket—preparing herself for the moment she would finally climb back into her mommy's heart.

"**Y**ou look beautiful," Joanna said to Renee. Renee spun away from the mirror, looking both surprised and embarrassed.

"I'm sorry. I didn't mean to startle you," Joanna apologized, as she stepped through the open door into Renee's room. "I just couldn't help noticing how nice you look." She also couldn't help noticing that the room looked as though a bomb had gone off in there. There were clothes strewn everywhere. But Joanna didn't comment on that. She understood well enough the feeling of not being able to find the right thing to wear.

"I feel like a jerk," Renee complained.

"Why?" Joanna asked, concerned.

"I don't know." Renee shrugged. "I guess I'm just not used to wearing a dress. I feel kind of like a linebacker in drag."

Joanna couldn't help laughing. It was such a ridiculous image. Renee looked nothing like a linebacker. "Well, you look more like a fashion plate," Joanna assured her.

But Renee didn't seem to take any comfort in

Joanna's opinion. "I really wish I didn't have to go on this stupid trip."

"It's not a stupid trip," Joanna protested. The counselors at school were treating all the exchange students to dinner and a show in New York. "I wish I were going."

"I wish you were too," Renee said.

Joanna was acutely aware of how dependent upon her Renee was becoming. "You're going to have a wonderful time," Joanna assured her.

"Are you sure I look all right?"

"You look perfect," Joanna said decisively. "That dress is very flattering on you." An idea suddenly occurred to Joanna. "You know, I have a necklace that would go perfectly with that dress. Let me go get it for you."

"No." Renee stopped her. "I already have a necklace to wear." She opened the velvet box that was sitting on her dresser and took out the silver locket. "Do you think this will look okay?" Renee asked, holding up the locket for Joanna's inspection.

"Let me see that." Joanna reached out to take it from Renee.

Renee laid the locket in the palm of Joanna's hand and waited for her reaction.

"Where did you get this?" Joanna asked, not taking her eyes off the locket.

"It belonged to my grandmother," Renee answered.

"This is an exquisite piece of jewelry," Joanna told her. "Is it an antique?"

"I guess so," Renee said. "My grandmother got it from her mother."

"It must be very special to you," Joanna said, handing the locket back to Renee.

"It is." Renee smiled. "Especially since there's a picture of my grandmother inside. Would you like to see her?" Renee opened the locket without waiting for Joanna's answer.

"She has a very kind face," Joanna said when she looked at the picture of the woman in the locket.

"She does," Renee agreed. "She was a very kind woman."

Was. The use of the past tense and the sad look on Renee's face told Joanna that Renee's grandmother was no longer alive. "I'm sorry," Joanna said, touching Renee's arm comfortingly.

"I miss her so much." Renee's lower lip began to tremble as she fought bravely to hold back the tears. "She's been gone so long that sometimes I have to look at her picture just to remind myself that she really existed, that my life with her wasn't just a dream."

"It seems as if you were very close to her." Joanna tried not to sound as though she was fishing for information—although she was. She knew very little about Renee's background. This might be an opportunity to get Renee to open up a little.

"She raised me." Renee smiled as if recalling fond memories. "Until she died." She snapped herself back into reality.

"When was that?" Joanna prodded.

"About six years ago," Renee answered.

"And then what happened?"

Renee let out a short, bitter laugh. "Then I had to go live with my mother, 'Lois the lush.' Or 'loaded Lois,' depending on which one of her friends you talk to."

More startling than the information was Renee's obvious hatred for her mother. Joanna had the horrible feeling that it was Renee's mother who was responsible for the scars Joanna had seen. She had to force herself not to jump to any conclusions. Not without more information. "Your mother is an alcoholic?" she asked as gently as she could.

"And a druggie. And a whole lot of other things you don't want to know about." Renee's answer came out sounding almost belligerent.

Joanna knew that Renee's anger was not directed toward her. "I'm sorry, Renee," she said simply, for lack of anything better to say.

"Please stop saying that," Renee implored. "I don't want you to be sorry. I don't want anybody feeling sorry for me. I don't want anybody's pity."

"I didn't say I felt sorry for you." Joanna tried to clarify her meaning to allow Renee some measure of pride. "Nobody could pity you. You're too strong for that. And too smart. And too pretty. You're an enviable person, Renee. Not a pitiable one. I don't feel sorry for you. I feel sorry for the things that have happened to you. There's a difference."

"It's hard to tell sometimes," Renee said wearily. "People love a good sob story. And when your life is as full of problems as mine has been, it gives 'em plenty to talk about. You don't know how many times I've heard people whisper 'poor child' behind my back. Maybe they mean well, but it doesn't come out that way. You see, my grandma always told me that I was gonna be great someday. But you know what? You can never be great when everybody else just thinks of you as a 'poor child.'"

"I don't think of you that way," Joanna told her, looking her straight in the eye. She could tell that Renee believed her. So Joanna decided to try and cross another bridge with Renee. "And Mallory doesn't think of you that way either."

Disbelief crossed Renee's face, but she didn't say anything.

"Mallory would give anything if you just allowed her to be your friend," Joanna went on. "You know, she's every bit as afraid of you as you are of her."

"She couldn't possibly be," Renee admitted, letting her guard down completely. "Not Mallory. She's smart, and beautiful, and everybody loves her. Believe me, she doesn't want to be wasting her time with me."

Poor child, Joanna thought. *Where did she ever get such misconceptions?* "Mallory would love to spend time with you, Renee," Joanna corrected her. "For instance, the day you went clothes shopping, Mallory really wanted to go along with you. Her feelings were hurt because you didn't let her go." Joanna hit a nerve.

Renee lowered her eyes contritely. "You know why?" she said in a voice just barely above a whisper. "Because I didn't really go clothes shopping. Do you want to know where I really went that day?"

The way Renee said it, Joanna was almost afraid to find out.

"I went to the zoo." Renee looked up at Joanna as if to try and read the reaction on her face.

But Joanna's only reaction was confusion. "The zoo?" she repeated.

"Yeah," Renee answered. "The zoo. I'd never been to a zoo before, and I really wanted to go. But I thought if I told anybody that, they'd laugh at me. So I went by myself."

"Oh, sweetie." Joanna didn't know whether to laugh or cry. "You should have told me. Do you know how much Mallory and I would have enjoyed a trip to the zoo? It would have been a wonderful day for all of us. And a chance for you and Mallory to start building a relationship, instead of building a wall between you."

Renee didn't say anything, but Joanna could see that she was getting through to her.

"Give Mallory a chance," Joanna requested.

Renee nodded obligingly. "I'll try."

"That's all I'm asking." Joanna smiled. "Nothing would make me happier than to see the two of you become great friends."

CHAPTER 34

Mallory sat by herself in the back booth of the deli, waiting for Kyle and Carolyn. It was Carolyn's birthday, and even though it was her day off, Kyle had been instructed to lure her to the deli so that everyone could sing "Happy Birthday," eat some cake, and give her a small gift.

Mallory was excited. She knew that it would be a surprise to Carolyn, who hadn't been working at the deli long enough to know that everybody got a little birthday celebration. Mallory was also looking forward to having a piece of Dennis's famous birthday cake.

"Here, I brought you another soda." Dee Ann plunked the glass down in front of Mallory as she passed by the table.

"Thank you, Dee Ann," Mallory called after her, more than a little confused by the gesture. She took a tiny sip, half expecting to taste something awful, Dee Ann's idea of a practical joke. But to her surprise, it was just plain old diet cola. Dee Ann had even put a wedge of lemon in the glass.

As Mallory sat there, sipping her soda,

wondering what had gotten into Dee Ann, she saw Kyle's car pull into the parking lot. Mallory jumped up and hollered through the kitchen door, "She's here."

The timing was perfect. Carolyn came through the front door just as Dennis carried the cake out of the kitchen singing "Happy Birthday." Everyone in the deli joined in, including the customers.

Carolyn was truly surprised. The instant she realized what was going on, she turned to Kyle and buried her face in his shoulder. And when she lifted her head again, Mallory could see that there were tears in her eyes.

"I can't believe you did this," Carolyn said when the song was finished. "You guys are the best."

"Make a wish and blow out the candles," C. J. told her.

Mallory was disappointed that her mother hadn't made it to the deli in time for the party. And she couldn't help feeling a little annoyed that it was because she was at home with Renee. She hoped Carolyn's feelings weren't hurt by her absence. Even Trudy had shown up, and she'd arranged to take the day off.

"I know just what to wish for," Carolyn said, smiling at Kyle. Then she closed her eyes and made her wish, just like a five-year-old, before blowing out the candles.

Everybody clapped as Dennis handed Carolyn a knife so that she could make the first cut. Then Dee Ann swiped the cake off the table.

"I'll take it in the back and cut it up," she told Carolyn. "It'll be less messy that way."

Mallory was stunned. She couldn't believe how thoughtful Dee Ann was being.

That was a change—a big change. But there was no time to think about Dee Ann. Mallory couldn't wait for Carolyn to open her present. Everyone in the deli had contributed, but it was Mallory who'd actually bought the gift. She knew it was perfect, even before she saw the look on Carolyn's face when she opened the box.

"They're beautiful," Carolyn gasped. She held up the earrings for everyone to see, as she shot a special smile in Mallory's direction.

"Let's see how they look." Mallory smiled back. She already knew they looked great. She'd told Carolyn as much the first time Carolyn held them up to her face in the department store, asking Mallory's opinion. Mallory had encouraged Carolyn to buy them then. But Carolyn had said they were way too expensive, way too extravagant.

"Great earrings," Dee Ann commented, as she started serving cake. "I hope everybody remembers that my birthday is November ninth."

"I almost forgot something," Trudy piped up. "There's a card too, girlie." Trudy handed it over.

Mallory half expected the envelope to say "girlie" on it. But what it did say was even more surprising.

"Carol N. Michaels?" Dee Ann said. "Hey, Trudy, I think you spelled her name wrong."

"No," Carolyn told her. "That's actually right."

"You mean your name's not Carolyn?" Kyle laughed.

"Not really," Carolyn answered.

"Then why do you call yourself Carolyn?" Dee Ann asked suspiciously. "I mean, if you're trying to have an assumed identity or something, don't you think you should pick a name that's not so close to your real name?"

Carolyn laughed at Dee Ann's suggestion. "I didn't exactly pick it," she explained. "It was a name that just sort of stuck. You see, at my last job, there were three Carols. And two of us had the same last initial. So we started using our middle initials. I was Carol N., which got slurred into Carolyn. And after a while, it kind of grew on me and I decided to keep it. Sounds crazy, huh?"

"Not crazy at all," Kyle said. "Huh, Mom?"

C. J. laughed. "You're not going to get any criticism from somebody who calls herself C. J., for Carol Joyce," she explained to Carolyn. "I must know two dozen women named Carol," she complained. "I wanted to be different."

"I can understand that," Carolyn sympathized.

Then she opened the card that was signed by everybody in the deli.

Those who weren't on duty sat down to enjoy the birthday cake. The others took theirs back to their stations after wishing Carolyn a happy birthday once again. Before long, the party dwindled to just Kyle, Carolyn, and Mallory. Carolyn got up to refill their sodas.

"So, were you really surprised?" Mallory asked as Carolyn put the sodas down on the table.

"Totally," Carolyn answered. "And these earrings are just too much. You are the best friend in the whole world, Mal."

"For real," Kyle said, looking into Mallory's eyes.

She held his gaze, feeling, for a brief moment, as though it were just the two of them again.

"Do you have any plans today, Mallory?" Carolyn's voice broke the moment.

Mallory was flustered, as if she'd been caught doing—or thinking—something she shouldn't. "No," she said, reaching for her soda. "No plans."

Mallory gulped down a good amount of soda before she realized that something wasn't right. The soda was awful, and it left a terrible aftertaste in her mouth. "What is this?" she gagged, putting the glass back down on the table.

"What's wrong?" Carolyn asked, with a look of concern on her face.

"There's something wrong with my soda," Mallory answered. "It doesn't taste right."

"There's nothing wrong with the soda," Kyle told her, picking up the glass from which Mallory had just drunk. He took a sip himself. "You picked up my glass by mistake. This one is my soda. And it tastes just fine."

"Oh, gross," Mallory said. "How can you drink that stuff? It's so sickeningly sweet; I'm afraid I'm gonna go into a sugar coma."

"Real men don't drink diet soda," Kyle joked, chugging down what was left in the glass.

"Why don't you spend the day with us?" Carolyn suggested, changing the subject abruptly.

"No way," Mallory protested. "It's your birthday. Don't the two of you want to be alone?"

"We're going out for a nice dinner tonight," Carolyn answered. "We don't have to spend the whole day alone together too. Besides, it *is* my birthday. So you have to do what I want to do. Right?" She looked to Kyle for verification.

"Right." He gave it to her.

"Are you sure?" Mallory was still skeptical.

"Absolutely!" Carolyn certainly sounded like she meant it.

"So what do you want to do?" Kyle asked. "See a movie?"

"That sounds good for starters," Carolyn answered, getting up from the table. "Let's go."

"I'll follow you guys in my car," Mallory said.

"I forgot that you came in your own car," Carolyn said. "Let's ditch it first, then we'll all go together."

"Okay." Mallory smiled, thinking how nice it was to have friends who didn't want to ditch *her*.

As the three of them headed for the door, Trudy stepped out from behind the deli counter and fell in line behind them.

"Going home, Trudy?" Mallory asked.

"Not just yet, girlie," Trudy told her. "I've got some important business to tend to first."

The way Trudy said it, it didn't sound to Mallory like it was pleasant "business," but she wasn't about to ask. And Trudy didn't seem ready to tell her either.

CHAPTER 35

Dee Ann checked the clock in the waitress station as she watched Mallory follow Kyle and Carolyn out of the restaurant. Time was definitely starting to tick away now, and Dee Ann was getting uptight. She had less than an hour to do what had to be done.

Dee Ann had wanted to take the day off so she could avoid this kind of time crunch. But thanks to Carol N. Michael's little birthday extravaganza, which conveniently happened to fall on Carolyn's day off, and Trudy's new mandate—that if Dee Ann went AWOL again, she'd be "dishonorably discharged"—Dee Ann had had to show up for work. And while she was sure that she had one "darn good, break-my-heart kind of a story," she wasn't about to tell it to Trudy. Nor was she about to call Trudy at the crack of dawn on the one day Trudy had decided to take off to hand her a line about needing the day off too. No. Trudy's senses were getting a little too keen when it came to Dee Ann. Dee Ann had been planning to attend Carolyn's birthday party anyway, because she hoped to see Joanna, but she wasn't planning to stay at the deli all day. No. Dee Ann had things to do. And she had to do them now.

Dee Ann headed into the kitchen with the intention of staging a dramatic exit from the deli, so that there would be no questions and absolutely no suspicion.

"Hey, Dennis," Dee Ann said sweetly as she stepped through the swinging doors. "The stupid soda machine is screwed up again. I can't get that twisty thing to work the right way."

Dennis sighed as he flipped one of the burgers he had on the grill, just the way Dee Ann knew he would.

The soda machine in the waitress station was constantly going on the fritz. Other than Trudy, Dennis was the only person in the place who knew how to adjust the "twisty thing" so that the machine would spit out the same amount of seltzer as it did syrup. It usually took him a good three or four minutes to do it.

"I keep telling Trudy we need a new machine," Dennis moaned as he headed out from behind the line. "But Trudy insists that as long as the 'twisty thing' works, there's no reason to spend the money."

"Yeah, I know," Dee Ann commiserated with him. "It's not so bad when it's slow in here like it is now. But when that stupid thing goes out while I've got, like, twelve tables waiting for drinks, I wanna cram that twisty thing right up Trudy's nose."

Dennis laughed. "Do me a favor, will you?" he asked as he headed for the swinging doors. "Keep your eye on the grill for me. Danny's on his break."

"Sure." Dee Ann smiled as Dennis headed out to fix the "twisty thing" Dee Ann had untwisted real good.

Other than the dishwasher, Dee Ann was alone in the kitchen—exactly the way she wanted to be. And while she would have found a way to "accidentally" stick her hand into the deep fryer with Dennis and Danny there, it was going to be a whole lot easier to do now, and a whole lot easier to control.

Dee Ann stepped behind the line and headed for the grill, pretending to keep her eye on it, just the way Dennis had asked her to. When she was sure the dishwasher was paying more attention to the dirty lunch dishes than he was to her, Dee Ann reached for the colander of french fries that were frying away. As she pretended to pull up the colander, she let the side of her left hand hit the surface of the bubbling oil, holding it there for three seconds flat. That was just enough time to make her own skin start bubbling away, so that it would look like she'd accidentally gotten a second-degree burn—a burn that would warrant a trip to the hospital.

But Dee Ann wasn't going to go to the hospital—even though she knew Dennis would insist upon it. While Dee Ann would assure Dennis that she would go immediately and offer to return to work if she could, she wouldn't. Dee Ann had suffered burns that were much worse. She knew this one wouldn't need any more "medical attention" than some aloe vera and a gauze wrap. But she was sure Dennis would fear the burn was much worse than it was and tell Dee Ann not to even think about coming back to work.

And he did.

Yeah. Dee Ann's exit from the deli was definitely dramatic. Before the curtain came all the way down, Dee Ann managed to grab one of the razor-sharp knives Trudy kept behind the meat counter so she'd have some kind of weapon in her good hand—just in case her timing was off.

CHAPTER

36

"Carolyn," Mallory whimpered. But all she got in response was a malicious laugh. "There is no Carol N. Michaels," Baby D told her. "Not anymore. So just forget all about her. Make believe she never existed. It's just you and me now."

"No," Mallory cried. No. No. No. It echoed over and over in her head. Her brain was frozen with panic, incapable of comprehending what was happening to her. She'd tried to stay calm, tried to figure a way out of this predicament. But it had quickly become apparent that there was no way out. The hopelessness of the situation was driving Mallory to the brink of insanity.

Mallory couldn't move a muscle. She was completely paralyzed, lying on the floor of an abandoned old shack, deep in the woods, far from help. It was no good to scream. More than no good. It was dangerous. Baby D had a knife, and she'd promised to use it if Mallory got out of line. It would hurt. Real bad. Because even though Mallory was paralyzed, she could still feel pain.

Baby D had proven that to her by pricking the tip of her finger with the knife. It hurt all right, and the worst part was that Mallory couldn't even pull back her hand. She was completely at the mercy of Baby D.

"Why are you doing this?" Mallory asked. She had to keep Baby D talking. There was nothing else to do but play for time. And pray for a miracle.

"I thought I just explained that to you," Baby D answered tersely.

Baby D had explained all kinds of things to Mallory. Wild, fantastical things. Things that couldn't possibly be true.

Why hadn't her mother ever told her about Baby D?

"Now for the sixty-four-thousand-dollar question," Baby D said, glaring down at Mallory. "Are we going to live like sisters? Or are you going to die like the rest of them? Your choice."

"Will you let Kyle go too?" Mallory asked. She couldn't see Kyle, but she knew that Baby D had him too. He was on the floor, across the room, paralyzed as Mallory was. Baby D had forbidden them to speak to one another. And to ensure Kyle's silence, she'd gagged him, saying that she had no reason to speak to him at all. She was interested only in Mallory.

But she didn't like Mallory's answer. Not one bit. "I shouldn't have even bothered to give you a chance," she snarled. Then she knelt down beside Mallory, brandishing her knife.

"No! Please!" Mallory begged.

"You think I'm going to kill you?" Baby D just laughed. "Oh, no. Not like this, anyway." She smiled at the knife in her hand. "You don't deserve to die like this. It would be too easy for you. Too painless. I want you to suffer. And while you're suffering, I want you to remember that I suffered more."

"What are you going to do to me?" Mallory sobbed.

"Well, right now I'm just gonna take a little souvenir." Baby D grabbed Mallory by the hair and lifted her head off the ground. Then she took her knife and started slicing away at the hair, cutting it so close that she actually nicked Mallory's scalp. When she finished, she got to her feet, holding the hair in her fist, displaying it proudly like a warrior with a fresh scalp. "Now you're Baby D." She laughed. "And I'm going home."

Baby D walked away from Mallory, out of her field of vision. But she kept right on talking. "Unfortunately, I can't send you to live with the Burnells. But I will take great comfort in the fact that you are going to die like the Burnells."

Mallory heard a splashing sound, as the overpowering odor of gasoline filled her nostrils.

"No!" she screamed at the top of her lungs.

"Go ahead and scream," Baby D told her. "Scream the way I screamed when they took *my* life away. It doesn't change a thing. The only difference between you and me is that *you're* never coming back. No, this time Baby D will be gone for good. Just like Baby B, and Baby R, and Baby K. And let's not forget Baby S over there. Yeah, pretty soon it'll be like you never even existed. And I'll be right back where I belong."

Baby D was looming over Mallory again. She struck a match and held it out for Mallory to see. "Just remember, this was your choice." Baby D tossed the match.

Mallory heard the *whoosh* as the gasoline ignited. "Please," she begged. "Please don't leave us here."

But Baby D ignored her. She just turned and walked away. And started singing. "In a cabin in the woods . . ."

The sound of her voice receded with her footsteps, until Mallory couldn't hear her anymore.

"Help!" Mallory screamed. "Somebody, please help us!" She knew it was futile. There was nobody to help them. She and Kyle were as good as dead. But she kept screaming anyway. It was all that she could do to fight for her life. And Kyle's.

Mallory wished that she could see Kyle. At

least that might be some comfort in their final moments. But all Mallory could see was the black smoke that billowed against the ceiling, getting thicker with each passing second. She lay there, helpless, watching the deadly gas accumulate, wondering how long she and Kyle could possibly last.

Outside, Trudy Zigler watched the flames skitter up the walls, wondering the very same thing.

CHAPTER 37

Dee Ann Watson climbed the front steps of Joanna Dunne's house even more emotionally battered than she was physically bruised. And Dee Ann was bruised real bad.

Dee Ann had had to fight for her life after all. While Dee Ann's timing had been nearly perfect, Snake's was impeccable. He'd called the deli to check up on Dee Ann not five minutes after Dee Ann had left. And while Dennis had informed Snake that Dee Ann was at the hospital having her hand attended to, Snake's sixth sense told him that Dee Ann was attending to something else. Snake had managed to arrive on the scene just as Dee Ann was trying to walk away from it.

At first, Dee Ann tried to reason with Snake. But Snake didn't want to hear about the sins of the past anymore. Snake didn't want to listen to the "poor, mistreated, little baby Dee saga" again. And he didn't want to hear about any plans for a future that didn't include him. As far as Snake was concerned, Dee Ann was eternally indebted to him, body and soul. After all, it was Snake who'd rescued Dee Ann from the life she wanted nothing to do with. He wasn't about to let her just walk away from the one he insisted she owed to him.

Dee Ann took the first blow to her face when she informed Snake that she didn't "owe" him a thing. Dee Ann had finally realized that the only person she "owed" anything to was herself. And while she knew she was putting her life on the line by pointing that out to Snake, she did it anyway, to prove to herself that she finally could.

The second blow had left Dee Ann lying face-down in the grass, struggling just to breathe. A part of her was grateful that she'd left Trudy's knife behind, because she knew Snake would have easily been able to turn it against her if she hesitated for even a second before plunging it into his heart—but she was also sorry that she didn't have an opportunity to do just that.

Because Snake managed to tear through Dee Ann's heart even without a knife. Yeah. Even the spur-studded heel of Snake's boot as he dug it into the center of Dee Ann's back wasn't as painful as the words he used.

Dee Ann wasn't going to have a "better life," because, according to Snake, Dee Ann was nothing more than a "piece of trash that even her mother couldn't love." Nobody was ever going to love Dee Ann, because Dee Ann wasn't worth loving. As far as Snake was concerned, Dee Ann wasn't even worth the bullet it would take him to blow her away.

Snake finally let Dee Ann go, insisting that Dee Ann would come crawling back to him before he even had a chance to finish his six-pack of beer. He managed to kill almost all the hope she was trying so hard to keep alive.

Yeah. Snake made it extremely difficult for Dee Ann to get in the car and head for Joanna's, because if Snake was right, if Joanna turned her away, she'd have no choice but to come crawling back.

And Dee Ann was willing to die before she'd let herself do that.

CHAPTER 38

Baby D pushed open the front door to her mommy's house without bothering to knock first. There was no reason to knock. There was no reason for Baby D to pretend that she was just a guest anymore—not in her own home. Baby D already had the set of house keys that rightfully belonged to her, the house keys the other baby should never have had.

"Who's there?"

Baby D heard her mommy's voice calling from the kitchen as she stepped through the front door into the foyer.

"Is that you, sweetheart?"

Baby D smiled as she closed and bolted the door behind her. And while she was dying to scream out and tell her mommy just who it was who really was home, she didn't. No. Baby D stayed quiet. Because Baby D didn't want to ruin the surprise. First she wanted to give her mommy her present. She could hardly wait to see the look on her mommy's face when she told her that she was finally home for good.

But as Baby D headed for the kitchen, her

mommy stepped around the corner, clearly startled by the sight of her.

"My goodness," her mommy gasped. "You scared me half to death."

"I'm sorry." Baby D's apology was sincere. "I didn't mean to scare you."

"It's okay." Her mommy laughed as she caught her breath. "I'm just glad it's you."

Baby D smiled, knowing that her mommy was nowhere near as glad as she would be.

"When I heard the door open," her mommy continued, "I thought that Mallory and Kyle were back."

Baby D had already covered herself with her mommy as far as Mallory and Kyle were concerned. Yeah. Baby D made sure she called home to ask for Kyle and Mallory long before the two of them lay burning. That way her mommy wouldn't suspect Baby D when neither of them ever came home again. As far as her mommy knew, Baby D hadn't seen Mallory or Kyle since the birthday party at the deli.

"When no one answered me I got nervous," her mommy went on. "I thought it might be a burglar. I was pretty sure I'd locked the door. I try to make it a habit when I'm home alone." Her mommy glanced at the bolted front door.

Baby D laughed at her mommy's overactive imagination. "It was just me."

Her mommy smiled. "And one beautiful-looking you, I might add."

"Really?" Baby D started to glow. "Do I really look pretty?"

"You look even prettier than pretty," her mommy assured her. "You know." Her mommy grinned. "I think this is the first time I've seen you in a dress."

"No," Baby D disagreed. "You've seen me in plenty of dresses before."

"I don't think so," her mommy said. "And if I have, they couldn't have been anywhere near as flattering as this one. I would have remembered."

"I used to wear one even prettier than this," Baby D reminded her mommy. "It was pink, with a little white collar and fluffy white sleeves," she told her. "Every time I lifted my arms, like this . . ." Baby D raised both her arms, "I had pretty little angel wings, remember?"

Her mommy just stared at her for a moment, looking a bit confused, before she finally let out a chuckle. "No. I definitely think I would have remembered seeing you in something like that."

Baby D had to fight the anger that was rising inside her. How could her mommy not remember her angel dress? Baby D remembered it. Yeah. Baby D remembered just how pretty her mommy had said she looked in it too. As Baby D stood there, struggling to hold back the tears that were threatening to surface, her mommy broke the uncomfortable silence between them.

"Well," her mommy said brightly, even though she still looked uncomfortable, "this one looks spectacular on you."

Baby D felt herself relax. "I bought it just for today," she admitted.

"It's beautiful," her mommy reiterated. "Only, aren't you a little early?" Her mommy glanced at her watch. "I thought you guys weren't leaving for another couple of hours."

"We're not," Baby D informed her. "I just wanted you to be the first one to see me, that's all."

An odd look crossed her mommy's face. "You did?"

Baby D nodded. "I wanted to surprise you."

"Well, you certainly did that." Her mommy laughed.

"No," Baby D started to clarify. "I mean, I *really* wanted to surprise you." Baby D held her mommy's present out in front of her for her mommy to take.

"What's this?" her mommy asked.

"It's a present," Baby D told her. "For you."

"For me?" Her mommy was surprised. "I thought you were the one who was supposed to be getting all the presents today."

"I am," Baby D assured her. "Only this one's for both of us."

Her mommy was clearly perplexed by the gesture. "You want me to open this?"

Baby D nodded excitedly. "Only don't rip the paper, you'll probably want to save it."

"Okay." Her mommy smiled as she headed back toward the kitchen. "Let me get some scissors then."

Baby D followed her mommy into the kitchen, anticipating the moment when her mommy would finally take her back into her arms . . . forever.

"This really is pretty paper," her mommy said as she started to carefully unwrap the box.

"I picked it out just for you."

Her mommy was still smiling as she lifted the lid of the box and pulled out the card Baby D had placed on top of the tissue paper. But as she started to read the words that Baby D had chosen so carefully, her expression began to change.

"May you always take comfort in the fact that the pain of the past now lies in the hearts of the monsters who tore yours apart—and joy in knowing that the future will lead us back around the moon and past the stars."

Baby D smiled excitedly at her mommy. But her mommy didn't smile back. No. Now her mommy wasn't smiling at all. In fact, the look on her mommy's face was not at all what Baby D was expecting. There was no trace of comfort or joy, only pain and confusion—as if the words themselves had ripped straight through her mommy's chest, tearing open the heart that Baby D was trying so desperately to repair.

"Open it up," Baby D said as her mommy stood staring at her, speechless. "You'll see. It's gonna make you really happy," she promised.

Baby D watched her mommy pull back the pink tissue paper and lift out the plastic bag containing the strands of beautiful blond hair she'd cut from Baby B.

"What is this?" Her mommy's tone mirrored the strained look on her face.

"The remains of Dr. Elaine Baxter's little girl," Baby D told her mommy proudly. "Her hair was almost as long as mine was before Calvin and Lorene chopped it all off."

This time, Baby D's words hit her mommy so hard, she seemed physically thrown a step back— away from Baby D.

"And this is Jack Riley's baby," Baby D said as she reached into the box and pulled out the second bag. "She was the easiest baby to get rid of. Jack Riley isn't getting an appeal either." She laughed.

Her mommy didn't move a muscle. She just stood there staring at Baby D.

"And Baby K," Baby D said as she produced the last bag in the box. "This is Judge Kramer's youngest son." Baby D smiled at her mommy. "You see? This is a good present."

Only Baby D's mommy didn't agree. No. Baby D's mommy didn't seem to be agreeing at all. Instead of opening her arms to Baby D, she wrapped them around her waist as if she might throw up.

"Who are you?" her mommy demanded in a tone that was anything but joyous and accepting. "And what in the world are you trying to pull?"

Baby D's heart started to break. Her mommy still wasn't seeing her. Her mommy wasn't even trying to see her. "It's me, Mommy." The tears started to well up in Baby D's eyes. "It's me."

"I'm not your mommy," Baby D's mommy said as she steadied herself against the kitchen counter.

"Yes, you are," Baby D told her as she reached into the box and pulled out the present she should have given her mommy first. "You are my mommy. The *only* mommy that's ever been in *my* heart."

Baby D held out the box for her mommy to open. But her mommy refused to take it from her.

"You see this ribbon?" Baby D asked as she carefully started to untie the shiny pink ribbon from around the box. "This is the ribbon you used to put in my hair," she told her mommy. "Remember?"

Her mommy put her hand to her mouth as if to stop the pain of the memory from escaping.

"And this is the ribbon I used to wear with my pretty pink angel dress."

Her mommy started to tremble.

"And this . . ." Baby D lifted the lid of the little jewelry box, "this is where you said I'd always be." Baby D pulled out her mommy's heart-shaped locket. "In your heart."

The sight of the locket filled her mommy's eyes with tears. And as Baby D opened the locket, placing it in the palm of her mommy's hand, her mommy started to cry.

"Baby Devon will always be in Mommy's heart." Baby D repeated the promise her mommy had made. *"Always."*

At the sound of those words, her mommy took in a sharp breath of air. It came out in a cry so wounded that it filled the entire room with the mournful echoes of the past.

"I'm home, Mommy." Baby D smiled. "I'm finally home."

CHAPTER 39

C. J. Stoddard stood frozen in disbelief, staring at the child who'd been torn from her arms eighteen years before. Baby D. Devon. The child she loved "around the moon and past the stars." The child whose screams echoed through her life.

But this was not Devon. In C. J.'s mind, and in C. J.'s heart, Devon Stoddard was dead. It had to be that way. Because it was the court's decision that C. J. never again see or be in touch with the baby she'd adopted. So when Devon Stoddard officially became Mary Jane Burnell, C. J. mourned the passing of her child. Devon Stoddard no longer existed. And C. J. had no choice but to accept the loss.

For eighteen years, C. J. had worked very hard not to think about Mary Jane Burnell. She had to remind herself that Mary Jane Burnell was not her child. She was not even entitled to speak to Mary Jane Burnell. To preserve her sanity, C. J. had to let Mary Jane go. All C. J. had left were the memories of her precious baby girl.

Devon Stoddard was preserved in C. J.'s heart,

forever three years old. Forever perfect. Forever innocent.

The young woman who stood in front of C. J. now was not her Devon. She was not even a ghost of Devon. She was some horrible aberration, a monster created by Lorene and Calvin Burnell.

C. J.'s head was swimming. She couldn't seem to get enough air into her lungs. The pain she felt was unendurable. And it surprised her. Up until that moment, C. J. was sure that there was no pain in the world to compare with the pain of losing a child. But she was wrong. This was worse.

The child that she'd lost had come back to her—not her child at all, but a murderer.

C. J.'s vision blurred. There was a loud ringing in her ears. Then the floor beneath her feet turned to Jell-O. With no will to fight what was happening to her, C. J. simply closed her eyes and surrendered consciousness.

CHAPTER 40

Baby D lifted her mommy's silver heart from the floor and placed it around her mommy's neck, where it belonged. Then she wrapped her arms around her mommy's limp torso and began dragging her through the kitchen and into the family room. The room where Baby D and her mommy played peek-a-boo and pat-a-cake. The room where Baby D cuddled up in her mommy's lap in the big old rocking chair her daddy had built for them, so that her mommy could rock Baby D to sleep while she sang her the rabbit song.

But now the rocking chair was gone. The walls that had once borne witness to Baby D's first words and steps, her birthday and Christmas, were now lined with memories that didn't belong to Baby D. Memories that Baby D would never be able to erase. And while Baby D tried to assure herself that the years ahead would be filled with the same kind of love and happiness, she had to struggle to hold back the pain of all the years that were forever lost to her.

Yeah. As Baby D lifted her mommy's body onto

the couch, she couldn't help grieving for the lifetime that had passed her by. The lifetime Kyle Stoddard got to live. The lifetime she wanted so desperately to have back.

Baby D didn't want to be all grown-up. Baby D wanted more than anything to be just a baby again. The baby her mommy would scoop up into her arms and hug tight. The baby her mommy would kiss and tickle and play happy games with. The baby that was always warm and safe and protected. The baby her mommy really and truly loved around the moon and past the stars.

"Mommy." Baby D started to cry as she slipped the knife she'd taken from the kitchen between the cushions of the couch and cuddled up next to her mommy's unconscious body. "I miss you so much."

Baby D pulled her mommy's arm tightly around her waist, snuggling up as close to her mommy as she could get. She wrapped her fingers around her mommy's heart even tighter, the way she used to do when she really was just a baby. In less than a moment's time, the pain of the years Baby D had been without her mommy suddenly dissolved. Every one of her senses seemed to be mercifully and joyously reawakened by the real sight, scent, and feel of being back in her mommy's arms. And as Baby D lay clinging desperately to the only person in the world she'd ever needed, feeling as warm and safe and protected as she had a lifetime ago, Baby D started to sing her mommy the rabbit song.

"In a cabin in the woods . . ."

C. J. Stoddard opened her eyes.

"A little old man by the window stood . . ."

Baby D smiled at her mommy, snuggling up even closer . . .

"Saw a rabbit hopping by ..."

C. J.'s entire body went rigid.

"Knocking at the door . . ."

Baby D wrapped the strands of her mommy's hair in her fingers, twirling it the way she used to when her mommy would sing her to sleep. "You sing it for me, Mommy," Baby D said sweetly, as if she were still three years old.

C. J. bolted upright, startled and horrified, pushing Baby D to the floor in a sudden knee-jerk reaction.

"Ooouch, Mommy," Baby D whined as she started to sit up. "You hurt me." Baby D began to cry like a three-year-old as she rubbed the side of her head. "You made me bump my head."

C. J. started to get up quickly, not to offer comfort to Baby D, but to move away from her. But Baby D wasn't about to let her mommy get away from her ever again. No. Baby D grabbed her mommy and pushed her back down . . . hard, pulling the knife from between the cushions of the sofa.

"Where are you going, Mommy? Don't you want to sing me the rabbit song?"

"Please," C. J. pleaded. "Please don't do this to me."

C. J.'s eyes were full of tears. But they weren't happy tears. They were tears of anguish, of regret, not relief.

"Don't do this *to* you?" As her anger rose, Baby D struggled to hang on to the child inside. "I'm doing this *for* you, Mommy," she corrected her, reaching out to stroke her mommy's hair gently. But as her mommy started to turn away, Baby D yanked the hair in her hand as hard as she could, turning her mommy's attention immediately back to where it should have been all along—on Baby D. "I did everything for you, Mommy," Baby D informed her. "Everything."

"Please don't say that," C. J. gasped.

"But it's true, Mommy," Baby D said as she made an *X* over her own heart with the knife in her hand. "Cross my heart and hope to die."

C. J. closed her eyes.

"Look at me, Mommy," Baby D demanded. "Why won't you look at me?"

C. J. just shook her head without opening her eyes.

"Look at me!" Baby D grabbed her mommy's face so hard, her mommy let out a cry of pain. "Don't make me hurt you, Mommy," Baby D cried. "Please don't make me hurt you."

C. J. didn't move a muscle.

"You've got to love me, Mommy." Baby D started to cry again. "You've got to."

C. J. cringed as Baby D laid her head in her mommy's lap.

"I promise you that if you don't let me back into your heart, I'll cut it right out of you." Baby D placed C. J.'s hand on her head, forcing C. J. to stroke her hair. "And then we'll both die, Mommy," Baby D sobbed. "I just can't live anymore without you."

"Okay." C. J.'s voice was filled more with fear than with reassurance. "It's going to be okay."

Baby D smiled at her mommy as she climbed up onto the couch, forcing her mommy to lay back down again so she could hold her.

"Besides," Baby D assured her as she pulled her mommy's arm back around her waist. "All the other babies are gone now. All except me."

The last little bit of color drained from C. J.'s face.

"I was pretty mad at you, Mommy," Baby D confessed. "Because I didn't get to have a better mommy while I was away. No. I got a mommy who didn't like me one bit."

C. J.'s chest started to heave violently.

"But now it's all better." Baby D took hold of the locket. "Isn't it, Mommy?"

CHAPTER 41

"Mallory!" Kyle's voice came to her from far away.

"Mallory!" It sounded like an echo.

"Mallory!" His voice kept tugging at her, pulling her out of the blackness.

She wished that he would leave her alone. Every time she became aware of his voice, she became aware, too, of the burning in her lungs, the throbbing in her head, and the searing pain in every muscle in her body.

"Mallory!" Kyle was shaking her now.

Mallory yelped in pain and pushed Kyle away from her. At least that's what she thought she did. In reality, she hadn't moved at all. She hadn't even opened her eyes.

"Please wake up," he begged. "Please be okay."

Poor Kyle, she thought. He sounded so sad, so frightened. She had to comfort him. "I'm okay," she tried to say. But she heard the sound that she made and realized that no words had escaped, only the tiniest murmur. And she didn't have the strength to try again. All she really wanted to do was let herself sink back into total blackness.

But Kyle wouldn't let her. "Oh, Mal." His voice was hoarse. "Please don't die."

For just an instant, it seemed a bizarre thing for Kyle to have said. She couldn't imagine what would make him think that she was going to die.

She struggled to open her eyes. But her eyelids were as heavy as lead.

"Help me!" The scream filled her head, but she could not will it to come out of her mouth.

She remembered the fire. And the smoke. Remembered that she was paralyzed. Remembered that she was going to die.

She felt hot tears stream from the corners of her eyes as her brain fought to reject the certainty of her fate.

"Don't cry." Kyle's voice soothed her as his fingers wiped the tears from her face.

She was startled by his touch, startled enough to open her eyes. The first thing she saw was Kyle, kneeling beside her. He wasn't paralyzed. He was okay. Just filthy with soot.

But there was no smoke, no fire. And they weren't in the cabin anymore. They were someplace much smaller, much darker.

Mallory's eyes darted around, trying to figure out where she was and how she'd gotten there.

"It's okay," Kyle told her. "We're safe." He didn't sound so sure of that. "For now, anyway."

"Where are we?" she managed to choke out, not believing the answer her own two eyes provided.

"In the deli van," he answered. "In front of my house."

"How did we get here?" she asked.

"Trudy," he told her. "Trudy brought us home."

CHAPTER 42

Trudy Zigler snapped open the barrel of her gun as she cautiously approached the front door of C. J.'s house. She checked to see that all the chambers were loaded before she carefully concealed her weapon in the small of her back under the waistband of her soot-covered pink jeans. And while Trudy prayed that she wouldn't have to use it, that the situation inside was already under some kind of control, she wouldn't hesitate to draw the gun if she had to. Yeah. Trudy Zigler would aim straight for the heart if that was what needed to be done.

Trudy glanced back at the van in the driveway, wondering whether she'd made the right decision. Leaving Mallory and Kyle unattended was a gamble, but Trudy knew she had no choice. Now she had to push Mallory and Kyle out of her thoughts so that she could focus all of her energy on securing what she hoped would be the final page in the scrapbook she desperately wanted to close for good.

Trudy reached for the handle of the front door,

hoping to find it unlocked. It wasn't. Trudy wasn't about to waste another minute trying to find one that was. She pulled off her windbreaker and wrapped it around her left hand and up her forearm. Then, with one sharp jab, Trudy put her fist through the stained glass window by the side of the door. She removed the jacket from her arm, then reached back through the broken glass for the dead bolt on the inside of the door. As she stepped into the foyer, Trudy placed her hand behind her back on the gun, in case her entrance hadn't gone unnoticed.

Fortunately, it had.

For a moment, Trudy stood silent. Her eyes scanned every inch of the balcony above her, listening for any movement from upstairs. When she was satisfied, she began to make her way as quietly as she could through the foyer and into the kitchen.

It was then that Trudy heard C. J.'s voice coming from the family room. The sound of it stopped Trudy dead in her tracks.

C. J. Stoddard was singing to the child she'd lost so long ago. But every word sounded so tortured and pained that Trudy's heart wrenched. Desperately, she fought off one of her "little spells." The fear of what she knew she would face inside that room was almost unbearable. But even worse was the deep sorrow she felt for the tragedy that could have been avoided. And it was a tragedy that could just as easily have befallen another nameless, faceless, helpless little girl who'd spent an entire childhood terrified of losing her mommy.

To this day, Trudy Zigler didn't even know what her "real" name was. Her conscious mind wouldn't allow her to remember that, or the names of the "parents" who had left her alongside the highway to die. "Trudy" was the name she'd chosen for herself, the name that belonged not to the woman who'd borne her, but to the woman who'd given her life—by offering her love, unconditional and unbounded. As far as Trudy was concerned, it was the woman who hadn't hesitated for a moment to open her arms to the child who was "so difficult to place" that was her "real" mom—from the very first day Trudy was placed in her care as a nameless, helpless five-year-old whose mind had mercifully allowed her to abandon her past.

And while Trudy considered "Zigler" her given name—the name that the kindest, most gentle man on earth wanted her to have—it hadn't become her legal name until she was old enough to sign the "proper paperwork." As far as the courts were concerned, Trudy was still bound to her biological parents, the people who had traumatized her so badly. And while Mr. and Mrs.

Joseph Zigler were granted "legal guardianship" over Trudy, they were never allowed to adopt her as their own.

As a result, Trudy spent her entire childhood terrified that one day the monsters of her past would crawl out of her nightmares and take her away from the mommy and daddy she loved. The mommy and daddy whose names Trudy would carry with her and hold sacred until the day she died.

As Trudy started to move toward the Stoddards' family room, steeling herself against the emotions she knew could cloud her judgment, she berated herself for not having figured it out sooner. Yeah. Trudy Zigler should have known all along just how much of a child's identity was tied to the name that child carried with it.

But Trudy hadn't figured it out until she filled out the birthday card she'd used as an excuse to come to the deli on the one day she told Joanna and C. J. she needed to take off.

Trudy had only shown up at the deli because she'd been following Kyle all day. She'd been sure that whoever was out there trying to avenge Baby D would plan to strike the child who'd replaced her on the anniversary of the day Baby D was taken away. And while Trudy's heart told her that Baby D was the only person on earth, other than Carol or Michael Stoddard, who could have possibly been so tormented by the past, she refused to believe it. No. Trudy wanted to believe there was some insane vigilante running loose. She had even suggested that theory to the police, right after the disappearance of Jack Riley's little girl.

But the police had brushed Trudy off, suggesting that she had "watched way too many Columbo movies." They insisted that there was no "Baby D" connection between the two disappearances, assuring Trudy that the paths of Elaine Baxter and Jack Riley had crossed numerous times in the courtroom over cases much more devastating than the one that was all but forgotten. And while they promised Trudy that they would "look into things," she knew that she would be just as forgotten to them as Baby D was to the people whose lives she'd set out to destroy.

The moment Trudy wrote the name "Carol N. Michaels" on the birthday card, she realized she should have listened to her heart. Yeah. It was Baby D herself who was trying to avenge her past. But Trudy wasn't about to let her destroy another life in the process.

As Trudy stepped into the family room, attracting the startled attention of both mother and child, she knew her only hope was to appeal to the fragmented pieces of the child Calvin and Lorene Burnell had managed to destroy long ago.

"In all my life," Trudy exclaimed. "I swear I thought I'd never live to see this day!"

Baby D bolted upright, nervous and confused. "What are you doing here, Trudy?"

"I wanted to be the very first one to welcome you home, Devon." Trudy smiled as she turned her attention to C. J. "You must be so happy to have your precious baby girl back."

The desperate look on C. J.'s face tore right through the little piece of Trudy's heart that wasn't already broken.

"What are you talking about?" Baby D couldn't hide the tension in her voice any more than she could the knife she was using to hold C. J. in place.

Trudy smiled. "You know just what I'm talking about. You'll never know just how much I prayed that you'd come home. We all did, didn't we, C. J.?"

"Yes." C. J. tried to fight back the tears as she told her child the truth. "We all prayed for you, Devon."

Trudy smiled at C. J. reassuringly, grateful that C. J. had somehow managed to find the strength to play out the scene Trudy knew was tearing her apart.

"You know who I am?" Baby D almost sounded excited.

"Of course I know who you are," Trudy assured her. "You're Carol and Michael's little girl." Trudy winked at Baby D. "Carol N. Michaels. That was very clever. I didn't figure it out until today. And when I did, I wanted to kick myself for not recognizing you sooner. But how could I have? You were just a baby the last time I set eyes on you, a beautiful, precious little baby."

Trudy could see that she was playing the scene the right way, because Baby D's eyes were starting to soften.

"You knew me when I was a baby?" Baby D smiled at Trudy.

"In a way," Trudy answered, suddenly pained by the faraway memory that flashed through her mind. "I even got to hold you once."

"When?" Baby D asked eagerly.

C. J.'s eyes seemed to be asking the same question.

"In Judge Kramer's chambers," Trudy answered.

Baby D's entire expression changed. Trudy prayed that she wasn't making a mistake by telling Baby D the truth.

"I used to clean the courthouse back then," Trudy explained. "And one day, when your mommy and daddy were in court fighting for you, Judge Kramer brought you into her chambers to talk to you. You were crying so much, you tried to run away, and you ran right into my legs. I scooped you up and held you in my arms for just a moment, a moment I'll never forget until the day I die."

Baby D's eyes welled up with tears.

"What happened to you and your mommy back then was a tragedy, Devon," Trudy continued to press on. "A tragedy that could just as easily have been my own."

Baby D's eyes stayed fixed on Trudy, as if she were trying to see into Trudy's soul.

"I had a bad mommy and daddy once too," Trudy told her. "A mommy and daddy who hurt me so much, I wouldn't even allow myself to think about who they were or what they did. But there were two people out there, just like C. J. and Michael Stoddard, who wanted to be my mommy and daddy. I was lucky enough to be able to stay with them from the time I was five until the time they died, even though they were never able to adopt me."

"My mommy wanted me to stay with her too," Baby D said. "But I wasn't allowed to."

Trudy nodded. "Every day I imagined the nightmare you had to live," she said. "I wonder, if the same thing had happened to me, if the bad mommy and daddy had stolen me away, whether I would have found the same kind of determination to survive as you did."

Baby D looked away. Trudy held her breath, hoping that she really had taken the right approach.

"You're lucky your bad mommy and daddy

didn't want you back," Baby D told her. "'Cause if they did, you'd have had to wait until you were all grown-up before you could kill 'em and go back to your real mommy and daddy."

C. J. closed her eyes as the tears streamed down her face.

"You did, didn't you?" Trudy tried to sound understanding. "You had to wait until you were all grown-up."

Baby D nodded. "'Cause if I didn't, some judge might have given me to people just as bad."

The last little piece of Trudy's heart fell apart.

"But now," Baby D told her, "nobody would even think about trying to take me away again. Now everybody knows how bad it is for a baby to be taken away from her mommy." Baby D pulled her hand out from behind C. J., tapping the blade into the palm of her other hand. "Isn't that right, Mommy?"

Trudy didn't take her eyes off the knife. She held her breath, hoping that C. J. would respond the right way.

And she did. "Yes, Devon. That's right."

"It sure is." Trudy wanted to draw Baby D's attention back to herself. "It's the worst thing that could ever happen to a child."

Baby D smiled up at Trudy.

And as Trudy looked into the eyes that seemed so distant and empty, she had to keep reminding herself that they belonged to the monster Calvin and Lorene Burnell had created. There was no way in the world Devon Stoddard still existed. Trudy was sure of it. Devon Stoddard had died a thousand painful deaths at the hands of Calvin and Lorene Burnell.

And while Baby D would always be in Trudy's heart, she knew she had no choice but to steel it against the child who'd returned. Yeah. She had to find a way to get the knife away from Baby D so that she could save the life of the mother who'd fought so hard to protect Baby D's.

CHAPTER 43

Kyle knew the instant he stepped into the room that he'd made a terrible mistake. He should have stayed in the van as Trudy had instructed him to do. But he couldn't stand the waiting. He had to make sure his mother was all right.

Baby D's face twisted in a look of unbearable anguish. "You're supposed to be dead," she screamed. In a flash she jumped to her feet and grabbed C. J. by the hair, holding the knife to her throat.

"Carolyn, no!" Kyle shouted.

"My name is not Carolyn," she reminded him. "It's Devon. Devon Stoddard."

"Devon, please," Trudy tried to reason with her.

"You shut up," Baby D snapped. "You saved his life, didn't you? You don't really care about me. Now you've ruined everything!"

Kyle could see the knife biting into his mother's flesh and the helpless, resigned look on her face. "Don't hurt her," he pleaded.

"She's *my* mommy," Baby D snarled. "You

can't have her anymore. Even if that means I have to kill her to take her away from you."

"You don't want to do that," he said as calmly as he could. He had to keep the situation under control, had to buy some time. "You don't want to hurt her. It's me you want." He took a step forward, offering himself in his mother's place.

"No!" C. J. cried.

"Stay where you are," Baby D warned, tugging hard on C. J.'s hair to quiet her.

But it didn't work. "Devon, don't listen to him," C. J. begged.

"What's the matter, Mommy?" Baby D baited her. "Aren't you willing to give up *this* baby?"

"I wasn't willing to give you up either," C. J. desperately defended herself. "I fought with everything I had. Michael and I both did. We nearly bankrupted ourselves, both emotionally and financially. And still we lost. If there had been anything else we could do, we would have done it. I would have done anything for you."

"Anything?" Baby D smiled with the same malice that dripped from her voice.

Kyle saw the look of horror that came over his mother's face.

"I want him out of our lives," Baby D demanded. "Forever."

"Over my dead body," C. J. said fiercely.

"That can be arranged," Baby D said cruelly,

pressing on the knife a little harder for emphasis.

Kyle knew that Baby D didn't really want to hurt his mother. But then, she hadn't wanted to harm Mallory either. Mallory was just an innocent bystander. If she hadn't drunk from Kyle's glass at the deli, accidentally swallowing the drug that was meant only for him, she wouldn't have been involved at all. And even then, Baby D had given Mallory the chance to save herself, but Mallory had refused to leave Kyle. Mallory had been willing to lay down her life for him, just as his mother was now.

But Mallory was safe, and with any luck, she had managed to call for help. Kyle had to protect his mother until that help arrived. He would do anything to accomplish that.

"Let her go and take me instead," Kyle suggested.

"No!" C. J. reiterated.

"Yes." Baby D smiled. "That's exactly what I'm gonna do. Walk toward me," she instructed him. "Very slowly."

As long as Baby D had a knife to his mother's throat, Kyle would do precisely as he was told. He moved very slowly, watching Baby D's face for approval at every step.

"Stop!" she told him after he'd gotten only about halfway across the room, not too far from where Trudy was standing.

Trudy hadn't made a sound or moved a muscle since Baby D had told her to shut up. And even though Trudy appeared to be looking down, Kyle saw that she was watching Baby D very carefully. He knew that Trudy was just biding time, the same way he was.

"Now move toward the wall," Baby D told him. "Over there, in front of me." Baby D's attention was focused completely on Kyle, as once again he obeyed.

Kyle was standing less than six feet away from Baby D. His mother stood between them, and he knew that any attempt to grab for the knife would only result in C. J.'s death. But if Baby D was planning to take Kyle, which was exactly what he was trying to lure her into doing, she would have to let his mother go first. Then he could put up a fight.

It wasn't a good plan. Kyle knew that the odds were strongly against him. He'd hoped to have heard police sirens by now. But there were none. There was no sign that help was coming. Kyle was on his own. He would have to do the best he could.

"Turn around," Baby D ordered him. "Put your hands against the wall. High. Where I can see them."

Kyle put both hands flat against the wall just a few inches above his head, turning his head so he could watch Baby D.

"Face the wall," she told him.

Reluctantly, Kyle began to turn his head, just as Baby D made her move. Kyle caught it out of the corner of his eye. This was the moment he'd been waiting for, his window of opportunity.

"Kyle!" C. J. screamed as Baby D threw her to the ground.

Kyle spun around to face Baby D.

Baby D had the knife raised and was lunging toward him, a split second away from plunging it into his chest.

A deafening blast tore through his horror and drowned out his mother's screams.

The fury on Baby D's face dissolved into confusion as the knife fell from her hand.

As Trudy stood poised, ready to fire again, the sound of sirens filled the air.

CHAPTER 44

The police called Trudy Zigler's actions "heroic." They were impressed by Trudy's efforts, particularly her "incredible marksmanship." But as Trudy stood watching the scene that was unfolding on the steps of C. J. Stoddard's house, as the police struggled to take Baby D away while a devastated Joanna Dunne wrapped her arms around C. J., Trudy wondered just how "heroic" her actions really were. Trudy was sure Baby D's bullet wound would heal, but she knew the emotional wounds would not. And as she stood there listening to Baby D screaming desperately for the one thing she wanted most in the world, Trudy had to wonder if she'd shown Baby D any mercy at all. For a split second, Trudy Zigler almost felt sorry that she hadn't had the heart to aim straight for Baby D's.

"Mommy!" Baby D cried.

Trudy wrapped her arms even more tightly around Mallory and Kyle and felt Dee Ann Watson clinging to the back of her shirt.

"Mommy, please!" cried Baby D. "Please don't let them take me away!"

Kyle couldn't hide the tears that Trudy knew he was trying desperately to fight back, while Mallory buried her head in Trudy's shoulder.

The moment unfolding before them was a repeat of the moment the cameras had captured so long ago. Only this time, there were no cameras or court-appointed vultures or curious onlookers. This time, there was no question as to what kind of justice was being served. Trudy knew there was no choice now but to let Baby D go for good.

"I want my mommy!"

With the strength of ten men, Baby D tore herself away from the grasp of the two officers who were struggling to get her down the front steps. Her hands had been cuffed in front of her because of her wound, allowing her to reach out for the locket that was still around C. J.'s neck. She ripped it off C. J. before the police regained their hold and tore her away.

"Baby D will always be in Mommy's heart!" Baby D screamed as two more officers lifted her feet off the ground to carry her to the squad car. "Always!"

C. J. Stoddard collapsed into Joanna Dunne's arms.

Trudy knew it was true. Baby D would always be in her mommy's heart.

"H ey, Mom." Dee Ann's voice cut through the deli. "Can I take my break now?"

Trudy looked up at the clock. "You've got fifteen minutes, girlie," Trudy told Dee Ann, trying to sound stern. But Mallory could see the smile tugging at the corners of Trudy's mouth, and the softness in her eyes.

"What a buster she is," Dee Ann said under her breath as she slid into the booth next to Renee. Kyle and Mallory sat across from them. "She's always on my back about something. This morning she made me scrub down the back of the deli van because the meat was dripping blood all over the place. She's neurotic about keeping everything 'shipshape.' It's like living with Mr. Clean," Dee Ann continued complaining about Trudy.

But she wasn't really complaining. In fact, Dee Ann was happier than Mallory had ever seen her—probably happier than she'd ever been in her life. Dee Ann had finally found what she'd been searching for—a real home, and a real mom.

Trudy had offered to take Dee Ann in after

she'd left Snake, and Dee Ann had accepted. She even accepted all the conditions that went with it. But she still liked to complain that living with Trudy was like living through boot camp.

Every time Mallory looked at Dee Ann, she couldn't help smiling at the wonderful change in her. Dee Ann was an incredibly pretty girl. And now, instead of trying to hide her good looks by being so shocking, Dee Ann was actually doing things to look attractive. She'd taken out the nose ring, and wore only one earring per ear. The combat boots were gone, and so was the purple lipstick. She'd even gotten her hair styled.

"Your hair looks really pretty, Dee Ann." Mallory complimented the new 'do.

"Yeah?" Dee Ann smiled, touching her hair. "You really think so?"

"Yeah, I do," Mallory assured her.

Kyle and Renee agreed.

"I got it cut just like yours," Dee Ann told Mallory. "I really like the way your hair looks short. I hope you don't mind that I copied it."

Mallory ran her hand through her short, short hair. Horrible memories began to surface, but Mallory beat them back. "Of course I don't mind," she said. "Except that I think you look a whole lot better than I do."

"Nah," Dee Ann protested. But she couldn't hide her appreciation of the compliment.

"You know, Mal," Kyle said, looking back and forth between Mallory and Dee Ann. "You may be right about that," he teased.

"Thanks a lot." Mallory backhanded him playfully, as both Dee Ann and Renee laughed.

"So what are you guys up to?" Dee Ann asked, changing the subject from herself.

"We were talking about going ice skating tonight," Mallory told her.

"I've never been," Renee admitted.

Mallory smiled warmly. She knew it was hard for Renee to talk about the things she'd missed out on, but every day, Renee was learning to open up more and more. She was learning to let go of the sorrows of the past and look toward a bright future.

They all were.

"You're gonna love ice skating," Dee Ann told Renee.

"Why don't you come with us?" Kyle invited Dee Ann.

"Really?" Dee Ann looked to Mallory and Renee for confirmation.

They both nodded enthusiastically. Really. Dee Ann was more than welcome.

"I'll have to ask Trudy, of course," Dee Ann told them. "But I'm sure it won't be a problem. She knows I won't get into any trouble as long as I'm with you. Hey, Mom," she called over her for a second, Mallory actually shivered.

"What's wrong?" Renee asked.

"Nothing," Mallory lied. "I just got a chill. That's all."

Kyle put his arm around Mallory and moved a little closer. "I'll warm you up," he joked.

But when Mallory looked into his eyes, she could see that he wasn't joking. It was as if he could read her mind, as if he were trying to protect her from the nightmare of what had happened to them.

It felt good having his arm around her, having him so close. But it was also strange, and a little frightening. The feelings she had for Kyle now were very new. And she was sure that Kyle returned them. They hadn't talked about them yet, so Mallory wasn't sure where those feelings would lead them.

But one thing was certain. Whatever happened from here, whatever direction their relationship took, Mallory was sure that she and Kyle would always be together.

shoulder to Trudy, who was behind the counter talking to C. J. and Joanna. "Is it okay if I go ice skating with these guys tonight?"

Trudy thought about it for a minute. "I don't see why not," she answered before continuing her conversation.

Joanna glanced over at Mallory and gave her a smile of approval. Mallory smiled back. Her mother had been right about Dee Ann. She'd also been right about Renee.

Mallory had learned something very important about her mother. Joanna's soft heart did not make her a weak, fragile person. Quite the contrary. Joanna's kindness and generosity of spirit gave strength to everybody around her.

All her life, Mallory had believed that C. J. was the stronger of the two women, but over the past few months, Mallory had seen just how much C. J. depended upon Joanna for support, and comfort, and strength.

With Joanna's help, C. J. had made it through the unthinkable. For the second time in her life, C. J. mourned Baby D. The psychiatrist now responsible for Baby D's care had recommended that C. J. have no contact with her—as much for C. J.'s sake as for Baby D's. Baby D's obsession with C. J. was not only unhealthy; it was dangerous.

A chill shot up Mallory's spine as she remembered just how dangerous Baby D was. And